Born Lucky
The JD Chronicles

By Christine Dougherty
www.christinedoughertybooks.com

Original Cover Art by:
Douglas Heusser

This book contains the beginning of
Faith Creation, All Lies Revealed,
Book One in the Faith Series

Available now. Look for *Faith* wherever you buy your
ebooks or on Amazon for the paperback.

* * *

Special thanks to the early readers, Chrissy, Bob, Mary,
Ann and Jim and to Debbie for the extra insight.
Thank you, Pauline Nolet, for proofreading and generally
keeping me on track; it is much appreciated.

* * *

This book is for my husband, Steve Dougherty,
because he has faith in me.
Love you, Biggie

* * *

Prologue

July 2010, The Pine Barrens, South Jersey

Gater Aronson brought the Ford pick-up to a rocking stop, tires sliding in the sand. The twin cones of the headlights picked out the twisted, light gray branches of wild blueberry bushes and the brown-black patched bark on the pines. Everything looked flat in the glare, like stage scenery. Just beyond where the headlights reached, shadows jumped in time with the lightly bouncing truck. A smoky cloud curled up before the headlights like gritty fog.

Gater was used to the dark woods at night, but he had an uneasy thought: why had he driven them *so* far back? They could have stopped a mile out from the main road just as easily as…what? four or five miles? more? How long had he been driving before he came across this little clearing? He found he couldn't really judge the distance; hadn't been paying enough attention. The seatbelt cutting across Mindy's boobs–making them look enormous–had distracted him.

Now he dialed up 93.3 on the radio, trying to chase out the willies. Blondie was singing about how the tide was high but she was holdin' on; wanting to be his number one. WMMR broadcast out of Philly so it was faint, fading in and out with an occasional burst of static as the radio waves traversed the twenty or so miles of pines between here and the city, but it was passable as long as he kept the volume turned low.

Mindy Gerber slipped out of her seatbelt and scooted down till her tailbone rested at the edge of the seat. She popped her flip-flopped feet up on the glove box. Then she crossed her arms.

"I'm not makin' out with you, Gater. You can just forget about that," she said. Her voice was tight, just shy of anger. Gater noted the ripple of unease that shook the last word, making it higher-pitched than the rest.

"Aw, come on, what are you scared of? Ain't nothin' out here gonna get you. I'll leave the headlights on, how 'bout that?" He stretched his arm out across the back of the bench seat, his hand just brushing Mindy's fluffy blonde hair where it had rucked up behind her head. He took in her pink-painted toenails, round calves, and smooth, suntanned thighs. Her jean shorts were short-short and her pink cotton underwear were peeking out under the curve of her buttocks. Her white blouse was a sleeveless middy, with a wide band of elastic tight to her trim little waist and the first three buttons unbuttoned, giving him an enticing view of the tops of her breasts.

Gater studied her like an engineer eyeballing a complicated run of pipes over a header. He can't figure how to get his arm around her. Her shoulders are too far down. Frustrating.

"Come on now, Mindy, take a look around. It's just the woods. Nobody here but us," he said, wiggling his eyebrows at her comically.

Mindy sat up, bouncing on the seat, her mouth a tight pout. "It's super trashy to make out in the woods. And in a pick-up truck! That's even trashier, Gater. You think I'm a hick, is that it?"

Gater moaned and tilted his head back against the seat. "Jesus jumped up, Mindy, you know I don't think you're a hick. Where do you want to make out, huh? At DeAngelo's like the eighth graders? We're in *high* school. We're seniors, just about; we can't be sitting there in a booth with slices in front of us swappin' spit while Tony pulls his pud behind the counter."

"Gater!" she said, bouncing again and reaching across to slap his arm. "That is dis*gust*ing!" But she is on the verge of laughing, too; he sees it and his grin widens. Everyone knows old Anthony DeAngelo is a pervert. And his pizza sucks, to boot, but there isn't a lot to choose from out in the boonies.

"You know what Mary told me?" Mindy said, "She heard he sneaks up into the drop ceiling and stares down the girls' blouses!"

"Which Mary? Grungo or Russo? 'Cause I can't see anyone going to any special effort to see down Mary's shirt."

Mindy slapped Gater's arm again, and he was gratified to see her breasts jiggle in the opening of her blouse.

"You stop that, she's my friend!" Mindy said. Then she leaned toward him, her hands on the seat in front of her. A

3

slow smile was sliding across her glittery pink lips as her breasts were pushed together in the tight V of her arms. Gater was mesmerized. He couldn't take his eyes off her. "Know what else she said? She said that he–"

The truck bounced roughly, the cab tilting back and up. As though someone had decided to jump on the back bumper.

Mindy let out a breathy little scream and Gater was glad she did because he figured (hoped) it covered the yelp that had jumped unbidden from his own throat.

"Oh, my Jesus, Gater," Mindy said, her voice a babble of rambling syllables. "I told you I hate these damn woods at night, what was that, is someone–"

Gater got himself together and put his hand over Mindy's mouth while flicking the radio knob down and dousing his headlights. "Shhh," he said, leaning low and pulling her down with him. Her lips were still moving under his hand, hot and sticky, and he felt himself getting hard, but he willed it away. *Don't want to get boner if we're about to get shot by some dipshit cranberry farmer*, he thought, and laughed nervously.

"What the hell is so funny?" Mindy asked in a furious whisper, pulling his hand away from her mouth.

"Aw, nothin'. Now just be quiet a sec and let me listen."

They both listened.

Gater heard nothing but the wind in the very tops of the pines, sighing. No crickets, no spring frogs, no cicadas. Weird. He opened his mouth to tell Mindy that everything was fine when the truck bounced again. Violently. The springs screeched and whoinged with the up and down movement. Gater reached to steady himself, his hand hitting the radio knob, and a burst of static blared through the cab of the truck. He hurriedly cranked the knob to off.

Mindy reached across the seat and grabbed at Gater's hands, scratching him by accident across the back of his wrist. There were tears glinting at her lower lids. In her fright, she looked about half her age–a grade school kid again. Gater was feeling kind of like a little kid, himself, and it made him angry. He sat up, pulling her with him.

"Christ, it's probably just Terry and them, trying to scare us. Probably rode out here on their quads. Fuckers." He squinted out into the woods, looking for any sign of the four wheel ATVs, but could see very little. The Barrens were dense with trees and underbrush. The sandy ground glowed in ghostly patches in the blue-black night.

"We'd have heard them if they were on their quads," Mindy said, her voice a shaky whisper. She wouldn't look out into the woods, afraid of the twisted and deformed trees she catches in her peripheral vision. Like monsters surrounding the truck. She kept her eyes on Gater.

"Yeah. But they might have parked a ways back and walked up on us. Douchebags." He had gripped onto the idea that Terry and John are fucking with him, but even before 'douchebags' is out of his mouth, he tries to remember if he told anyone he was bringing Mindy out here tonight.

Mindy was right, they would have heard the high-pitched quads–that distinctive, buzzing whine of the ATV engines–if they'd been anywhere close by.

"Did you tell anyone we were coming out here?" he asked and Mindy shook her head, blinking.

"Just my mom," she said, as tears overflowed her lash line and coursed down her cheeks.

"Okay, okay, take it easy, we'll just get the fuck out of here and–" he'd been turning himself forward, reaching for the keys dangling from the ignition while he talked. As his fingers grazed them, the truck bounced again, the back end seeming to come off the ground entirely, sending his face into the steering wheel and Mindy crashing sideways into the dashboard.

The truck bucked front to back over and over as though it had come alive, a demonic metal bull straight from the pits of some hellish rodeo. He turned to Mindy, dazed, and watched as she was flung between the dash and the back of the seat, her arms out to steady herself. She was screaming and her eyes were tightly closed, as if she were on a roller coaster. The glove box popped open and everything flew out. His owner's manual, the insurance card, pens...Mindy screamed and screamed. He reached for her, yelling "Mindy, take my hands, hang on, Mindy–" but she kept screaming, trying to brace herself, getting purchase then slipping as the truck bounced and rocked.

Then she was looking at him, wide-eyed. "Your face, your face!" she screamed, and Gater felt the hot wetness that had burst from his nose, and with that realization, the pain set in. He knew right away that his nose was broken because he'd seen his friend Sean's nose get broken once when they'd all been twelve. Sean had fallen into the handlebars of his bike. It had been bloody as hell, but he'd had been okay.

Just like I'll be okay, Gater thought, *soon as I get us the fuck out of here.*

He reached for her, yelling over the screeching of the springs. "It's okay, I think my nose is broken, but I'm okay! Hang on, hang on–"

Abruptly the truck stopped bucking. They froze, huddled together on the middle of the seat, instinctively bent low beneath the windows. Mindy's eyes, red and teary and round with panic, were locked onto Gater's face. She wanted him to fix this, fix this, get them out of here, she wanted her mom and her dad, she wanted her daddy to fix this…she wasn't aware that she was saying 'fix this fix this' over and over, out loud. Like a chant. An incantation.

"Mindy! Be quiet!" he said, his voice low and choked. The fear–the terror–in his voice silenced her. She became aware of a chuffing, breathy sound somewhere behind the truck, almost like a laugh. But there was no humor in it. There was another chuff, deepening to a moan, from the front, and then an answering grunt from the back.

Mindy's arms rashed out in goose bumps.

Like a conversation, Mindy thought. They're talking to each other. But what the hell–

Gater's eyebrows pulled down and he tilted his head–she knows he hears it too and is just as puzzled by it. Then her eyes stray past Gater to his door, and she sees that the lock button is up. Strong, cold hands squeezed her stomach.

His door was unlocked.

She reached past him, fingers straining. She touched the lock with the tip of one shaking finger when the door burst open outward. She shrieked and threw herself back toward the passenger door, as Gater was pulled out the driver's side door, bouncing and screaming, his mouth a black hole of panic. A half moon crescent of blood stained the edge of the seat where his chin hit it.

At the last second, his hand caught the steering wheel, his knuckles white with strain as he is pulled backwards. Mindy reached for him, shrieking in terror, but the wheels turn in the soft sand and the steering wheel twists abruptly, shaking him loose.

Mindy threw herself forward across the seat, still shrieking, reaching for where his hand had been a split second before. Gater was dragged along the sand into a dense stand of bushes, further into the dark. He was still screaming. His eyes were enormous with fright, the lower half of his face black and shiny with blood from his broken nose.

He reached for her with one hand while the other clawed helplessly at the loose sand.

He disappeared into the underbrush.

There was a crack, like a large tree branch breaking, and Gater's scream was cut off.

She realized she was still yelling his name and she bit down on her lip, cutting her shrieks to breathy whimpers. She reached for the door handle. She had to lean way out, into the black night. The crazily disturbed swirls of sand glow whitely where Gater had been dragged into the tangle of bushes. Her shaking fingertips bumped the door and it sprang open farther, creaking, and she yelped in panic. Then her hand connected with the cool metal handle, gripping it, and she pulled roughly, throwing herself back across the seat. The door closed with a bang and she slammed down the lock button with a sob of relief.

She sat back, shaking, wrapping her arms around herself. She listened.

Her eyes strained to see into the black woods.

Nothing. No noise, no movement. Her shaking began to subside. She looked to the ignition. The keys were still there.

Relief, like a cool washcloth on her forehead, calmed her racing thoughts. *Okay, it's okay, I can just drive out, get help for Gater, bring help back, get daddy, daddy can fix this…*

She slid behind the steering wheel, checking the door

lock again, compulsively pushing it down just to be sure. In her panic, the passenger side door slipped her mind.

Shaking, she reached for the key and turned it. The truck engine ground lifelessly. Unaware she is doing it, she laughed, even as fresh tears rolled down her cheeks. She shook her head in denial and turned the key again and from the engine, nothing but the low rurr rurr rurr of a dying battery.

"No…oh, no," she said.

She let her hand drop from the key and closed her eyes, trying to compose herself. She couldn't seem to get her thoughts ordered and she had to, if she was going to get out of this.

The night had gone quiet again…no wind, no frogs or crickets; just deep, untouched stillness.

She tipped her head into her hands, squeezing her eyes closed, trying to think.

The passenger door clunked and swung slowly open, creaking on its hinges. The chuffing sound rolled into the cab, seeming to run up her right side like a hot tongue, and she froze. Her eyes opened with reluctance and she stared blindly out the windshield, paralyzed with fear. The hair at the back of her neck rose.

She began to turn her head. The chuffing became a grunt. There was an answering grunt outside the driver's side window.

It seemed to take forever to do this one little thing, to accomplish this tiny movement, to just turn her head and look...

But she did it. She finally got there.

And then she screamed.

Christine Dougherty

-1-

WHERE ARE GATER AND MINDY?

by Sandy Mancini

Eakintown Shout Out, July 6, 2010

Still no sign of George 'Gater' Aronson and Mindy Gerber, who were reported missing by their parents on Monday, July 4.

Occasionally people get lost in the woods and it seems that might be the most likely (and optimistic?) conclusion to draw regarding the disappearance of the popular, local high school couple, Gater Aronson and Mindy Gerber.

George Aronson Sr. and Michael Gerber reported their children missing late in the day on July 4th when they hadn't yet returned from a night out on July 3rd. According to sources close to Michael Gerber, his daughter had told her mother that she and Gater were 'going wheeling in the Barrens' (a popular term among the kids that can mean anything from actual 4x4ing to merely driving the many trails that criss-cross the Pine Barrens south and east of our town).

On the morning of the 4th, when the children had not returned home, George and Michael took Michael's truck and drove Route 71 to some of the more likely trailheads in search of Gater and Mindy. For the people on the Opinion Page this past week saying that the families should have contacted the authorities immediately, please pay heed: it is not uncommon, especially during more strenuous 4x4ing, that a vehicle might get stuck (bogged down) in a sandy area, or get a flat tire, or an engine might die if it becomes overloaded with mud or water. Most of the residents of Eakintown have had experience with this with our own children (or even ourselves!) to know that it happens quite frequently and though it might make for an uncomfortable night and a long walk out, it is most usually not an indicator of catastrophic danger.

It was in this spirit of mild concern that George and Michael set out to look for their children, expecting to find them at any moment, probably on foot, certainly shamefaced, and no doubt tired and hungry. As the morning wound into late afternoon and they still hadn't located the kids nor found any sign of Gater's F150, they became more seriously concerned. In the meantime, Regina Aronson and MaryEllen Gerber had been at home calling every child in the town who might have an idea where Gater and Mindy had gone.

All to no avail.

Joy turned to fear when the truck belonging to Gater was found, but with no trace of the missing children.

On July 5th, Gater's truck was located and brought out by Park Rangers working in coordination with the State Police. Sources have indicated that there were 'areas of concern' relating to what forensics have found in the truck, and although they are keeping the families informed, they've yet to make a public statement.

A source close to the Gerbers has stated that finding the truck with its battery dead at first elated both families as it seemed a clear sign of why Gater and Mindy hadn't stayed with the vehicle. But that elation has turned to dread as no further sign of the children has since emerged.

Neither Gater nor Mindy was known as flighty or the least bit at odds with their families. A source close to George Aronson has indicated that George has expressed full confidence that Gater would have navigated his way out of the Barrens, had he been given the opportunity.

No one could have expected that they would seem to have simply vanished.

Dear Aronson and Gerber families, our thoughts and prayers are with you.

If you get the opportunity this week or next, try and stop by the Aronsons and Gerbers households with a word or two of encouragement. Offer what you can, whether it is your time or simply your prayers, and we'll all help pull through this like the good neighbors we know each other to be.

And as always, this is your friend Sandy sayin' "I'll see you where the news is!"

Christine Dougherty

-2-

I sure don't do these things to myself, no matter what anyone else might think. Take this newspaper clipping for example: you think I shoved it under my own door? Not a chance. Listen, I feel bad for the kids and their parents, of course I do, but there isn't anything *I* can do about it. I'm staying put this time. I need a break, too, you know. I don't have to go dragging out after every weird little thing that happens out there, do I?

Do I?

Christine Dougherty

-3-

My name is John David, but everyone calls me JD. You can, too, if you want. My aunt Mayella used to tell me I was born lucky. If she were alive today, I think she'd have a padded room somewhere down from mine; that's how crazy she was. Not that my room is actually padded, but a mental hospital *is* still a mental hospital, after all.

Born lucky...oh, man, do I ever beg to differ on that one. I'm not a glass is half empty kind of guy in general; I try and stay upbeat, but still. I gotta call it like I see it.

Here's what happened, according to what I've been told:

My parents lived out in the boondoggles, way out in Pennsylvania, practically off the grid. They were smart people. Dad had an engineering degree, and he was also some kind of math genius. He was gone a lot, but when he was home, he was *really* home. He didn't work a nine to five kind of job; he'd be gone for a month or three, working, but then he'd be home for a month or more straight. It must have been some kind of contract work or something; Aunt Mayella was never a hundred percent clear on what it was he was doing. So she said.

Aunt Mayella was my mom's sister.

Mom was a painter. I don't mean like a hobby painter, she was a full-blown artist with gallery shows and celebrities purchasing her canvases…the whole enchilada. If I told you her name, you'd be able to Google her and then you'd see. She was a very well respected, sought after artist.

They had me when they were both older–in their fifties. I was their only kid. I was born on December 5ᵗʰ, 1985. Sometimes I imagine the world shivered that night, a goose walking over its collective grave.

I was only three days old when they died.

From what I understand, it was pretty spectacular. Their house, a big log cabin, exploded. And I don't mean like, gas line exploded. I mean, exploded like a professional demolition crew had gone in and wired everything up with bundles of C4. I mean, flattened right down to the scorched earth. Beams and timbers whittled down to toothpick-sized bits of char. The sand in the soil around the house had morphed into shards of glass. You know how much heat it takes to turn sand to glass? Right around 3000 degrees. There aren't many things that get that hot.

My parents were incinerated in seconds.

I, on the other hand, was blown clear of the apocalypse.

Oh yeah, you heard me right. Blown right clear of it. Baby in a baby seat in the woods one hundred feet from the house. The investigators said it must have been just the right set of circumstances. The chances of everything happening in the *exact right way* to save my life that night were probably somewhere in the realm of winning the lottery every week for a year.

The investigators kept the baby seat I'd been in. The underside was a melted ruin, according to what they told Mayella, but the rest of it was in fine shape. It was found canted over, almost sideways in the snow, about two hours after the fire crews got there.

One lonely news van had found its way to my parents' house by then. The reporter had needed to take a leak after their last take, and because it was an hour ride back to the station, he'd gone into the woods to do it. That's when he came across my car seat. He said I wasn't even crying; he just happened to see the blanket moving in the dark. It had scared him, actually, and he said he'd assumed it was an animal, raccoon or something, and he'd bent to pick up a rock, ready to peg me with it.

He'd lifted the edge of the blanket, arm pulled back with the rock at the ready, but it had just been me. He said I was hanging from the little harness, sucking my thumb. Not a care in the world was how he put it.

Just a dumb baby that didn't even know it had lost its parents.

He didn't put in the dumb baby part, that's me. That reporter and I have stayed in touch and we've talked it over many times. I like hearing the story, actually.

The reporter's name is Dex Hammond. If you're from the tri-state area, then you probably recognize it. He was twenty-five when he found me; just starting out. Now he's fifty and one of the faces people trust into their houses with the news every night. *I* don't get to see him on television because this hospital tunes to another station during the news. Us loonies can't handle the news, I guess.

But he still visits me all the time. I guess he's kind of the dad I never had.

So that's where Aunt Mayella got the 'born lucky' stuff. Three days old and blown clear of whatever force it was that leveled my parents and their house.

"Yes, Aunt Mayella," I used to say, "I'm just *really* lucky."

-4-

Okay, so anyway, this clipping. The article about Gater and Mindy…first of all, it makes you reconsider nicknames, right? I mean really, Gater? Did the kid love alligators or what? If you ignore that part though, it really is troubling.

I know the area they're talking about. It's actually not far from here, from the hospital, I mean. We share the same stretch of Pine Barrens as the town those kids were–are–from. The Pine Barrens are big, acreage wise, but people don't get lost in there. This is a fact, by the way. Since recorded history, not a single human being has gotten irretrievably lost in the Pine Barrens. Unless they wanted to, of course, but that would be a different story. And I can tell you that isn't the story of Gater and Mindy.

You can tell from the article that they were good kids from good families. Just the fact that the parents didn't get the police involved right away tells you that much. They assumed that they'd be able to locate the kids with ease. No thought to runaways or any sort of foul play. The worst they probably conjured was the kids stuck in a rolled truck. But there is something more here…something that travels to me seemingly through osmosis.

I had been hovering over the clipping, reading, but unwilling to touch it. The problem was that the bottom had been folded over, not allowing me access to the end of the story. Tricky, tricky. The messenger knows me well enough, then.

I shuffled nervously around and around it, my slippers whispering across the hard surface of the industrial floor. Then I knelt near it and leaned way over, trying to peek into the folded-over section, but no luck. I sighed and lowered my head.

I'd have to touch it.

I didn't have a choice.

I picked the clipping up and I see…

… *Sandy Mancini, the woman who wrote the article. In the produce department of a grocery store. She is weighing the difference in price between two kinds of apples. The one she likes better was more expensive and she is debating with herself…the age-old question of quantity versus quality…*

See, this is the majority of everyone's life…strings of numbingly boring moments strung together to make a whole. Occasional fun things or exciting things get thrown in, but mostly it's blah, blah, blah.

When I 'see' other people's lives, it's not like seeing a movie. Not at all. Most lives could really benefit from a writer, actually. Amp up the action, humor, charm…

Take Sandy for example. Still there, debating apples. I wish this 'talent' of mine were reciprocal in some way. If she could only see me, hovering an inch or two over the Gala in her hand, then I could yell:

"Buy the ones you like best! You're not going to live forever, you know!"

Well. But she'd probably run screaming from the supermarket, half out of her mind. I've had a long time to get used to this. I've never met someone else who could do it.

But back to the clipping. I close down the window with Sandy, wishing her the best. I know how fulfilling a dull life is; believe me, I know. I keep it as dull as possible around here. Why do you think I choose to live in a mental institution? You might think it would be exciting to live around the loonies, but everything is very tightly controlled…wake time, breakfast time, craft time, lunch time, TV time, bed time…nothing happens off schedule. Ever. Hardly ever.

I love it.

Clipping, clipping, right, gotcha. I'm on it. I rub the newsprint between fingers and thumb, thinking then not thinking, and I turn to look out my window. The light is bright, too bright, I squint my eyes closed…

…*Gater and Mindy are in the dark cab of a truck*…

My eyes pop open again. I'm not sure how or why it works. I can understand seeing the woman who wrote the article. But shouldn't I be able to see the pressman who ran it? The kid who delivered it? Most importantly, the sneak who clipped it and shoved it under my door? So, yeah, I don't know why it works this way, but sometimes I can see through clippings. Right through to the real story underneath.

I go to my chair, next to my bed, and stare out the window again. The clipping is in my hand, but I hold it lightly this time. It's really bright outside. A gardener stands from the Azaleas where he has been weeding and wipes a red and black bandana across his forehead. You can tell it's hot out. It must have been hot that night, too. Hot and dark in the woods where…

…the sun has gone down. Mosquitoes. Deer flies. Wind in the pines. The leather of the truck seat. Blondie singing about the tide. A beautiful high school girl is talking to me but I can't hear what she's saying. Her eyes sparkle with laughter, and she is so cute, so incredibly, almost innocently sexy. This must be Mindy. She leans nearer to me. Is she going to kiss me? God, I hope so. Fear fills her eyes as the truck tilts violently. It pitches and heaves. I see the steering wheel loom large and then a flash of bright pain…

I open my eyes back in my room. My hand goes to my nose. Ouch. He broke it for sure. Poor Gater.

I stand and go to the mirror. A small runnel of blood is dribbling over my lip. My nose hurts. Not broken but certainly bruised. Luckily I wasn't that far in.

It's rough, being a sympathetic psychic.

See why I didn't want to touch that clipping?

See now?

-5-

There is a light tapping on my door but I don't say anything; I know who's on the other side. That's not from being psychic, either. I just know Nora Buchanan very well by now. She can only wait so long after seeding the bait.

She'd be terrible as a trapper.

"Come in, Nora," I say, but she doesn't even need that; she's halfway in by the time her name drops from my mouth. She is tall, six feet in her sensibly tan, two-inch pumps. She is blonde and more handsome than pretty, and she's physically imposing. Her looks and strength have served her very well over the years. She runs this hospital, Shaded Pines, and I've heard she handles patients and underlings alike with the same strong hand.

She glances from the clipping on the floor near the chair to my nose, and she grimaces. She knows what this process can do to me.

"You saw something," she says. A statement, not a question.

I nod and turn to the bed to sit. Nora takes the chair, crossing her legs at the ankles and tucking them under. Her suit is very pretty: summer weight cream, a few shades lighter than the shoes. Her blouse is a light swirl of color…flowers or maybe a paisley.

Nora is the facilitator of my stay at Shaded Pines, and for that, I am eternally grateful to her. But now that Aunt Mayella is dead, Nora is the only one who knows the extent of my talent, and I get irritated when she springs these little 'tasks' on me. She knows better than anyone how really dangerous it can be. She knows why I hide from it.

She reads all this on my face.

"JD, I'm sorry, I really am. These kids…it's terrible that they're missing. I can't imagine what their parents are going through, and I just thought, with you being so close by and all…do you want some ice for your nose?"

I shake my head, a bit ashamed. I am pretty certain that, whatever befell Gater, ice will never fix it.

"No, of course not," I say, sighing. "But you could just ask me to read these things, you know? Instead of ambushing me. Give me a fighting chance, at least, to prepare myself."

A smile appears on her face. *A wry twist*, as Aunt Mayella would have called it. It is my turn to know what she is thinking and to be honest, she's right. If she'd tried to hand me the clipping directly, it would have been an hour (at least) of wrangling on her part to get me to read it. As she'd done it, my curiosity had gotten the best of me.

A word here about my curiosity: it is insatiable. Once I get a firm hold on something, I cannot let it rest. Take the Gater and Mindy thing for example…reluctant as I started out, I am locked in, now. Wild horses and all that, you know what I mean? It's probably the thing I hate the most about myself–the thing that seems the most contradictory to my otherwise sedentary nature.

I swing my legs up onto the bed and put my arms behind my head. In my peripheral vision, I see Nora dig a small note-book and tiny golf pencil from her pocket. She sits, pencil and pad at the ready.

"I don't have very much," I start, "but what I have is dis-tressing. Very distressing. They were out in the Pines and I can't tell you anything about location. It's all too much one thing out there." I glance at Nora, and she is nodding as she writes. She knows what I mean. "There was something vio-lent, a violent event that shook the whole truck. Shook might not even be the right word…that truck was thrown, in a sense. Almost like it was being tossed around on a wave. A person couldn't do that."

I close my eyes and look at the memory of Mindy lean-ing in to kiss me. I slow it down and watch her lips move. Something with a *sh…she…she said…*then the tip of Mindy's pink tongue…the or that?…*that…she said that he…*and then the jolt. I freeze the memory.

Mindy's mouth is just beginning to open, her eyes half-filled with fear. Her gaze has slid slightly to her left. That's where the tilt started–at the back. The back end tilted down. Far enough down that the back bumper must have been in the sand. It was after this that it had snapped forward and begun to buck.

I know that Gater was thrown into the steering wheel, but it wasn't at that second. It wasn't as the truck began its crazy gyrations; it had to have happened a bit later. This is common, too. The impressions I get can be jumbled, run together. I think it's because these are not necessarily impressions I am getting from the people involved, it's more like a video tape of someone's memory and sometimes it's faulty. Whole parts are missing or, even worse, bent over on each other, making it a confused jumble.

I try and see past the 'paused' Mindy to the window behind her. I can only see what Gater saw, but I can at least try and see anything that registered with him…anything he might have seen out of the corner of his eye, say, or glanced at by accident. If it's in his brain, I should be able to get to it. Maybe.

There is a rough blur at the far edge of the passenger window behind Mindy. I focus on this blur.

I imagine a tiny man in a black suit sitting squarely in the middle of my brain. He squints at the image projected across the inside of my forehead. Leaning forward, he whispers '*enhance*' and a scurry of unseen technicians start twisting dials and adjusting lights and darks. I always find it amusing to imagine this scenario; it's something I've picked up from the handful of espionage movies I've seen.

But even though it is amusing, it also *works*. At least, some of the time.

Now I keep my eyes trained on that blur. It is a lightish gray brown, only a bit lighter than the darkness it's surrounded by. Could this be someone running past the side of the truck? Could this be the perpetrator?

Enhance…

The overall shape of it lightens more and stands out against the black. It's almost a head and shoulder shape but the 'head' part is grossly misshapen and the 'shoulder' part shrunken and twisted. It doesn't look…well…human.

Back in my bed, in my real self, I frown.

There is a blackish bit about halfway down the top bulge of the area I think of as the head. What is that?

Enhance…

It sharpens and comes slightly more into focus.

It is an eye.

Christine Dougherty

-6-

I snap forward and open my eyes, my arms coming from behind my head.

"Jesus," I say, my breath hitching in my diaphragm.

Nora sits forward.

"What was it JD, what did you see out there?"

I don't say anything; just let her sit in anticipation. That relentlessly forward jutting face of hers gets on my nerves. I know I am getting angry for all the wrong reasons. It's the agitation from being out of myself. Mostly I am trying to make *less* of what I just saw. It could have been a person, maybe a friend, harassing them. It might have nothing to do with the broken nose and the disappearance. Nothing at all.

Except, of course, I know that isn't the case, don't I?

"I don't know what it was. The truck was shaken, or...bounced would be a better word. It bounced up and down as if a giant kid were playing rough with it. Then...something...ran past the passenger side window. It was...it was gray, darkish gray and really...kind of misshapen."

"Misshapen? How?" Nora asks, her interest really piqued now.

"I don't know Nora, it was just...not...human shaped. Okay?" Now I am extremely irritated. I really don't want any part of this, and I certainly don't want to hear what she is going to say next.

"We have to contact the authorities," she says.

At 'we' I was already shaking my head. I knew where she was going; I *should* know…because it's where she *always* goes–the *authorities*. I've dealt with the authorities before and you know what? Thanks, but no thanks. But Nora is a rule follower, a t crosser, an i dotter. She believes in systems and checks and balances and laws. Good for her, somebody has to. But not me.

"I'll contact them," she says now, "I won't get you involved."

I roll my eyes at her.

"Really? And tell them what? To search the Barrens for something misshapen? Come on, Nora. If you call them, you know they're going to want to come here. They're going to want to talk to me. I can't do it. I won't do it."

There is a certain mindset with any law enforcement person I've ever dealt with and here it is in a nutshell: they laugh at me before an investigation and then after I give them some piece of information that helps them solve a case, they *still* want to laugh at me. The difference being that after I help them solve a case, they laugh and say that what I provided didn't help them at all.

And they are very disdainful.

It's that part that I can't stand anymore.

I shake my head.

"Nope," I say. "I'm not doing it."

Nora sits back and folds her arms over her chest, her blazer lapels scrunching up.

"Nora, I'm not. Forget it. For...get...it."

I shake my head and stare hard at my bathrobed lap.

Silence.

She's good at this. Good at waiting out the crazies.

"But JD...you didn't see them get killed, right? Or feel it?" she says, breaking her silence.

"No. But that doesn't mean they weren't," I say.

"What if they're still out there? Gosh, their poor parents, you know?" Now she is staring past me out the window.

Mindy's face flashes into my mind, young and pretty and innocent. So much in love with (me) Gater. So happy.

"Nora, dammit," I say. But I'm weakening, and she knows it. She's an old hand at breaking through defenses.

"I'll call them now," she says and stands. Despair washes over me, and I lower my forehead into my hands and close my eyes. Then her hand is on my shoulder. "I know it's hard for you, JD. I wouldn't ask if it wasn't important...if their lives weren't at stake. You know that, don't you?"

I nod, not raising my head. I do know it. I do.

But that doesn't make it any easier.

Christine Dougherty

-7-

The Trooper shifts, leather belt and boots squeaking. The chair is tight for him. Not that he's fat, no state trooper is fat, he's just big. A really big guy.

He tilts his hat back on his head and wipes his big thumb across his brow. It's also very warm in here. I'm not sure why they keep the heat so high. Possibly to give lethargy a helping hand. Or maybe some of these zombies have stopped generating their own body heat. They should lay them out on the solarium tables like lizards sunning on rocks.

Now he yawns then glances quickly at me.

"Sorry," he says. "It's just…it's so hot in here."

I nod. I don't give him more than that. He's been here a half hour already, but I still don't know where his head's at.

He had introduced himself as Trooper Raymond Stiles when Nora brought him in. He'd looked at my bathrobe and slippers and then taken in my room without comment. He'd probably seen much, much worse on his way up here. I may be too skinny with a ridiculous amount of heavy black hair falling down over my face, but at least I'm not a drooler, or a screamer, or the worst…a crier.

"Well," he flips his little notebook closed. "We'll look into it."

He rises, creaking anew, and puts a hand out. My hand is

more or less swallowed in his. He glances over his shoulder to where Nora stands, leaning against the wall. She smiles, but it is tight.

"He really can help you, you know," she says, and I feel embarrassed for her and for me. Mostly for me. I know what it must look like. I mean, I live in a *mental hospital* and I'm claiming psychic abilities. Maybe I should just declare my sovereignty over France while I'm at it.

Trooper Stiles nods and his features cloud. He has dropped my hand.

"I hear you, ma'am, it's just that I'm not sure what to do with this information. I mean, it's not really even a location, right? We're already sure that they were in the Barrens. That's where we found the truck. What we need to know is where the kids went from there. Where they are now."

I am nodding, and I force disappointment into my features.

"That's what I said, too," I say to the Trooper, but really I'm saying it for Nora's benefit. "What I saw doesn't do you any good, does it? Well…it's too bad. I really would have liked to help."

Now I smile and cross my hands behind my back. Nora's features have drawn down to a suspicious squint, and I widen my smile at her.

The Trooper looks at me. I don't sense any suspicion, contempt or even pity from this guy…and that's not the norm, believe me. There is something stoic about him, without the grimness. He's the type that, once he's on your side, he's staying there. No matter what. He's a comforting sort of person.

"I appreciate your desire to help. I wish there was something..." he trails off, shaking his big trooper head.

"Well, I guess that's that then," I say, stepping toward the door, trying to kind of usher him out. "If I think of anything else then we'll call you, but chances are, you know, that I won't. I mean, it's really more of a *contact* thing, if you get me, so, it's too bad, but..."

The Trooper had started toward the doorway, nodding, then he stopped and turned back to me.

"A contact thing?" he asks, eyebrows together.

"Uh, yeah, you know..." I rub my fingertips and thumb together to demonstrate. "I have to touch something to get a picture."

"And you got that little bit you saw from a newspaper clipping that neither of the missing kids had ever touched?"

His tone seems doubtful and that puts me on the defensive.

"Well, yeah, and I saw the lady who wrote it, too. It's not, like, an *exact science* or anything. I can't explain it or justify it, okay?"

He glances at Nora and then back to me.

"I'm not doubting you, it's just that...well, I think there might be something else you can do...if your doctor here says it's all right."

My stomach drops, and I automatically start shaking my head. Oh no. No way. No *way* am I sitting in that truck. To be completely surrounded by that kind of crap energy? No, thank you. I know that's what he's going to suggest.

But he surprises me.

"Maybe if I took you out there...out in the Barrens where we found the truck?"

Is he kidding?

He continues, "You could feel around a little...see if you can pick up their trail."

I am shaking my head with renewed energy and backing away. The backs of my knees hit the bed and I sit, the bed springs protesting.

"No. No way. I'm not going out there."

"JD, just listen to him for a second, maybe–" Nora says, taking a step into the room.

I hold my hand up to her, palm out, cutting her off.

"No way, Nora. Forget it. The woods? Who's the crazy one now?" My face is hot with both aggravation and fear. Nora knows better than anyone that I hate even the thought of being in the woods. The isolation. The silence. Or worse, what if they aren't silent? What if I were to hear branches cracking and furtive woodland creatures shuffling about, planning to do me harm? Nora has said time and again that she thinks this phobia of mine is directly related to what happened to me as a baby, that I must have retained some fearful instinct from associating the blast with the woods. I don't know about that. When Dex tells me the story of finding me out there on that December night, he describes a pretty content little baby hanging in that seat. He never says anything about the baby being distressed or bitten or even freezing; the blanket covering the car seat must have served as a kind of igloo, keeping me warm.

I don't know. I don't remember it.

The Trooper has stepped back and his features register surprise. Outside of the psychic stuff, I'd probably seemed relatively normal until my little outburst. Now that I'm waving my freak flag, he'll be pretty quick out the door.

But guess what? He surprises me again.

He walks across the room and sits back in the chair across from my bed. Our knees are nearly touching. I look at his big gray knees across from my skinny sticks in light blue pajamas. He really is a big dude.

"JD," he says, "How about this? I'll take you out there and we'll just try. No big deal. If it's too much, I bring you back here. But I think that you'll be okay. And I'll be with you…what could possibly go wrong with me there?"

He's right, you know? I mean, geez, just look at his belt! He's got a gun, big flashlight, handcuffs and some kind of little tube–probably pepper spray. He's right, he's one hundred percent right. There is nothing in the woods of Southern

New Jersey that could get past his defenses. We don't even have bears around here. I heard about someone getting killed by a deer one time, but I'm gonna guess that's a pretty fluky occurrence. And I never looked it up to see if it was even true.

I nod my head, but reluctantly. I glance up at him.

"Okay," I say. "Okay, I'll *try*…I'll try."

He nods, too, and puts his hand out.

"That's a deal, JD. You have my word on it," he says, dropping my hand and standing. "Okay, you ready to go?"

He wants to go right now? I was picturing tomorrow, maybe the day after. Although I realize that doesn't make much sense. It's already July 7th…they've been gone for three days now.

So. I stand up, too.

"Yes, okay. Just let me get changed."

Nora and the Trooper exit my room, Nora pulling the door closed behind her. I start digging in my closet for clothing suitable for both the Barrens *and* a sudden onset panic attack—in other words—something as durable as it is comfortable.

-*8*-

Trooper cars are pretty nice to ride in, did you know that? I don't mean crunched into the back, either. I imagine that would be quite uncomfortable for a number of reasons.

I bounce around on the seat a little, glance in the back, glance out my window. People are of two types, I observe, when you pass them in an official vehicle: the first group glances at the car with casual curiosity, continuing on with whatever they were up to; the second group (much larger than the first) stares dead ahead with two hands on the wheel, seemingly frozen in place. Interesting dynamic. I wonder which type of driver I would be–casual or uptight? I probably won't find out any time soon since I don't drive. I'm more of a passenger by nature, a scenery watcher.

"We're going out past Eak to Homesburg where the Ranger station is," Trooper Stiles says. "I contacted them while you were getting changed…a few Rangers are taking us in. They have their own Jeeps for the trails."

Eak is what locals call Eakintown, and it's the town where Gater and Mindy lived. Live, I mean. May as well stay positive.

I don't like the idea of more authority-types. I got lucky with Trooper Stiles, but most of them aren't as accepting–unless he's just really, really good at hiding his contempt.

I pull my phone from my pocket. It's an iPhone that Dex

gave me on my last birthday; my 25th. I'm not surprised that there's no signal. Although we aren't more than an hour from a major city, Philadelphia, we're still pretty remote, technology wise. There are people out here who don't even have access to cable.

We're at the Ranger station in less than fifteen minutes. The station is small–a cinderblock building roughly two hundred or so square feet inside. This is where they sell camping and fishing permits. I had been in it once when I was six and Dex wanted to take me canoeing. The trip never really got off the ground, so to speak. The only moisture our canoe saw was my embarrassed tears as we rode shamefully back to the rental place in the back of a pick-up, the big yellow canoe hanging over me like shame, itself.

I don't tell the Trooper about that trip. Besides, I reason with myself, you're not six anymore.

Although it's a sunny day, full-on summer sunny, it's gloomy out here in the Barrens. It is pine trees as far as the eye can see. Female white Gypsy moths hang from the trunks as their brown mates flit stupidly, zigzagging randomly until they happen upon them. The white females will lay eggs and then die, never having moved from the spot they selected after emerging from their caterpillar cocoon. They fall to the pine needle carpet below like a drift of snow in the wrong season. That sad fall is their only flight.

Cicadas buzz their fire-house alarm, rising and falling

through the octaves. The sound is equally unnerving and annoying, seeming to drill into your head with its insectile whine. I think it could drive you to the brink of insanity, if you listened too long and too hard.

The woods themselves are dense and murky. The pine trees are–in a word–ugly. Great, towering sticks, their branches pointing straight out from their sides, they have an almost laddered appearance. The forest floor is a tangle of sticky Mountain Laurel and wild blueberry bushes with pale gray, ghostly limbs.

And it is *humid*. Humidity so thick, the air itself is like a hot, spongy animal tongue, wrapping you and calling out the moisture in your body. The least exertion causes a flop sweat so intense that your hair is swimming pool wet within five minutes, which, in turn, calls to the mosquitoes and black flies as the Sirens were said to have called to squalid sailors of lore.

In case you haven't noticed, here's a news flash: I don't like the woods.

And not to prejudge, but I don't think I'm going to like the Rangers, either.

They're standing beside a Jeep as we turn into the dirt lot. They're both blond, short, and heavy boned in their khaki shirts and green shorts and their faces are impassive, but it's the impassivity of people who were talking about you when you walk into the room. They cross their arms over their chests with a synchronicity that looks rehearsed. There's something disorienting about them, but in my agitated state, it slips past me.

Trooper Stiles parks and looks over at me.

"Doing all right?"

I nod, my eyes sliding back to the Rangers.

"Funny, huh?" the Trooper says and I turn to him, my head cocked.

"What's funny?"

He nods, indicating the Rangers.

"They're twins. You didn't notice?"

Oh, yeah, I think, twins. That was the disorienting thing. I nod.

"Okay, well, let's get this show on the road," he says and exits the car. It first lowers and then springs back up, relieved of his weight, and I am tossed side to side. That, too, is disorienting in its seafaring feeling. Nausea begins a slow burn at the bottom of my stomach.

The Rangers have come forward and they both shake the Trooper's hand. There is a rumble of conversation too low for me to hear from inside the car, and all three turn to look at me.

This is it, I think, time to get out of the car...you're looking pretty idiotic right about now...pretty psycho...just get out of the car.

I get out of the car.

My feet hit the dirt parking lot. The cicada shrill seems to crescendo as I stand and my knees shake in its staccato rhythm.

I am in the woods.

Christine Dougherty

-9-

The Rangers come forward like curious yellow Labradors. Now that I have pinpointed what was disorienting about them, they no longer seem hostile–actually, quite the opposite in their dog-like, friendly eagerness.

"Hi. I'm Andrew," one of them says, hand out to me. As I shake his hand, the other one comes forward, his hand out-thrust, nearly bunting his twin aside.

"I'm Jackson," he says and takes a turn mangling my fingers.

"Really?" I say. "Andrew and Jackson? Andrew Jackson?"

They laugh and their laugh is a bit animally, too, a bit barnyard. Kind of a cross between a bovine low and a jack-ass bray. OoooooohHAW! OoooooohHAW!

Yikes.

The door of the Ranger station opens and a young woman comes out. There's no other way to put this: she is stunningly beautiful. Her hair is a dark flood over her shoulders and her eyes are almond-shaped and deeply black. She has a foreign, dusky quality that seems to speak to some latent, middle-eastern heritage. The Ranger uniform looks entirely different on her, its blandness highlighting her exotic features, rather than dampening them down as you might think they would.

She nods to the Rangers and Trooper and then she turns to me.

"I've heard about you, JD," she says. "I'm True." She reaches out and after the briefest hesitation, I take her hand.

There is a small ripple that passes between us where our hands are linked, and I look into her eyes. Her pupils expand, and suddenly, I am somewhere else...

... darkness and pain and a dark-haired little girl, maybe two or three, huddled in a corner, crying, terrified of her own tears because any sound will bring the monster back. The monster is, she is, she is...

I step back sharply and drop her hand.

"Your name isn't True," I say; my voice is quiet, barely above a whisper. I am dazed by the intensity of fear and potential violence I witnessed.

She shakes her head, but not in negation.

"No, it's not, or rather, it *is*; *now* it is. I changed it when I turned seventeen." She tilts her head, her hair picking up what little sun gets through the pines; it shines almost blue-black. "It used to be Trudy. How did you know?"

She is remarkably undisturbed.

This has happened to me before, of course. Sometimes physical contact with someone will give me a flash into his or her world, but it doesn't happen very often and even if it does happen, with long-term association the chances of it happening fade. It is almost like I develop an immunity to anyone who remains in my life. Probably it's something born of necessity–I wouldn't want to have a psychic burst every time Dex and I shake hands or every time Nora hugs me. It would become exhausting.

I don't say anything right away, I'm a little too disturbed by what I 'saw'. Strangely, she smiles. It is just a small smile and tinged with sadness, as though she is somehow aware of what I've seen in her past. It occurs to me that it might be in my eyes and on my face; that it might be obvious, at least to her.

I am about to answer her when she glances past me, something at the opening to the parking lot catching her eye.

I turn to see a man on a horse, clip clopping into the lot. The horse is brown and on the smallish side–even I can see that–but its chest is wide and deep and its legs are stocky and muscular. The man is a perfect match for the horse. He is somewhere in his mid to late fifties with a body like a wooden barrel, and his Ranger hat has been modified to accommodate a wide raven's feather tied with a braid of leather.

"Roger!" True says. She grabs my hand and gives it a quick squeeze–no visions this time–and then she is past me and running a hand over the horse's nose, smiling up at Roger. "You're coming, too?"

He nods and tips his hat to her.

"That I am," he says, and dismounts. It's not a quick process but it is dignified in its own way with its feeling of effort and determination.

"Hi, boys," he says to Andrew, Jackson, and Trooper Stiles and then he walks to me. The horse saunters along at Roger's heel looking like the world's biggest dog. "I'm Roger," he says, his hand out. I put my hand in his and the then the horse's nose is on my hand, blowing hot and soft. Large chin whiskers tickle my hand. "Pepper likes you," Roger says. "That goes a long way with me."

I look past him to True and she smiles into my eyes.

Sometimes, when I get a psychic flash from someone, I'll have a strong sense of knowing them, a strong bond. I feel it with True, but here's something else: I think she feels a bond with me, too. But she's not psychic as far as I can tell…so, where would her feeling of attraction to me come from? It's almost as though she just *liked* me at first glance. I don't understand it.

Roger turns and addresses everyone at once.

"We headed in?"

Trooper Stiles nods and sets his hat more firmly on his head. Andrew and Jackson nod in unison and cross their arms over their chests. Suddenly, True is next to me, and in my peripheral vision, I see her nod.

Now they're all staring at me.

I nod, too, and try to smile. Okay, I think, what could go wrong with all these people around me? But a small worm of unease squeezes up into my consciousness.

Hope I didn't just jinx myself.

Christine Dougherty

-10-

Andrew and Jackson take the lead Jeep with Trooper Stiles riding in the back seat. I'm sitting next to True in the Jeep she is piloting and Roger brings up the rear on Pepper. I twist back to see him and the horse.

"Is that horse state-issued?" I ask.

She laughs. "No, although Roger campaigned heavily to get her on board as an official Ranger…you know, like police dogs and police horses are actually members of their departments?" I nod and she continues. "It really would be a good idea, I mean, one thing we're concerned with out here is the quality of the environment, and you really can't get more eco-friendly than a horse, can you?"

"No, I guess not," I say, turning to face forward. The Jeeps are completely open, nothing between us and the world save a roll-bar over out heads. The trees and brush became thicker as soon as we turned onto the trail. I have a deep, claustrophobic itch in the back of my mind. I can't let it get further than it is right now; can't let it become a cyclical, self-defeating, all-encompassing obsession. I try and concentrate on other things.

"The trail is really smooth," I say, "I thought it would be bumpier."

"It will get worse further in. Nothing heart-stopping, but

we'll certainly start to pitch and bounce a little more once we're in there." She smiles at me; just a quick glance and then she turns her attention back to her driving. I am struck again by the deepness of her eyes. "Don't worry, okay? We'll be fine. The most dangerous thing in these woods are the mosquitoes. Besides, we're not going that far in."

"I thought the truck was found really deep in the Barrens," I say.

"It was found about five miles in on a pretty well-traveled trail. That might seem like a good distance if you aren't used to these woods, but believe me, there's a lot more to them than that." She glances at me again. "Did you know you can go all the way from here to the ocean and never leave the Barrens? You can get all the way to Delaware, too. These woods are bigger than most people think."

We ride for a while in silence, the Jeep growling along. The clip clop of Pepper's hooves comes to me faintly through the thick air. "But no one has ever gotten lost in them, right? That's what I read. That's a fact, isn't it?"

She doesn't say anything for a minute. We're beginning to bounce more as the trail roughens. Sunlight dapples greenly onto the dirt and sand around us.

Man, is it ever hot. I wipe my forehead on my sleeve and wait for her to respond; I don't feel the need to push for the answer to this particular question.

"According to the books on the Barrens, no…no one has

ever become permanently lost in here. Everyone is found..."
She shakes her head and her jaw tightens. "They're just not
always found alive."

"I thought you said there's nothing dangerous out here?"
Fear is trying to force its way back up to the forefront of my
mind...I push it back, but it takes two hands and all my
weight to make it go.

"The most dangerous thing out here is the people. The
most dangerous thing to people is their own panic, fear, stu-
pidity..." She trails off and I'm about to ask her a question
when she speaks again. Her voice is firm but it holds an eerie,
otherworldly quality, like someone speaking to you from the
past–or the grave. "Everything is survivable," she says, "As
long as you have the will to survive it."

I shiver involuntarily and consider her profile. I already
know that she has lived through something most likely un-
survivable to many people; I know it from what I saw when
I shook her hand. I open my mouth to speak, but before I can
get the words out, a deep chill courses through me, momentarily freezing my blood in my veins while my head feels like
it's on fire. I don't feel this way very often. I think I know
what True is going to say next.

"We're here."

And so we are.

***

We're pulling in behind the lead Jeep. Andrew and Jackson have already gotten out and Trooper Stiles is struggling himself from the back seat. Roger and Pepper arrive at True's door. I am aware of them all, but only peripherally.

There is something here that has grabbed my attention: a large, overwhelming energy. You might think that, coupled with my unreasoning fear of the woods, I'd be twice as terrified by now, but you'd be wrong. This kind of psychic overload piques my curiosity and I have an irresistible sense of discovery, or rather, of something that is crying out to be discovered. It must be how a spelunker feels at the entrance to a new cave.

I exit the Jeep and Trooper Stiles has come to meet me.

"This is where they–"

I brush past him, barely hearing, and kneel abruptly at a tangled cluster of blueberry bushes. I can of course sense the shock radiating from the people behind me. I put a cap on that energy and then ignore it. I turn my full attention to the ground before me.

I see each white grain of sand, each fallen pine needle and leaf. Small sticks and a beetle carcass don't miss my inspection and a sand funnel spider peeks out from the bottom of his trap and then retreats.

I put my hand on the sand and nothing happens. As I told the Trooper, this is not an exact science; I'm never entirely sure how or even *if* a vision will occur. I sit back on my haunches and take a breath. I'm not clearing my mind or anything like that, I don't have to; I'm in it. I'm just looking for the connection. Not *willing* it, I can't do that. It's more of a coaxing.

I lean forward again and put both hands in the sand right under the brush line. The sand is gritty and slightly cooler in the shade. I dig my fingers in, searching for at least one grain that was in contact with...who? With Gater? With Mindy? I don't know yet...

I feel a sharp tug at my ankles. What the hell? My first thought is that one of the Rangers has grabbed me for some reason and I glance back...but they are all standing a short distance away, watching me. I'm careful not to register their expressions. I don't care–don't *want* to care–what they think right now.

There is still pressure on my ankles even though they're all at least ten feet away. Not real, then...it's part of whatever happened that night.

This must be something felt by Gater or Mindy. Most likely Gater, I think, for no good reason. I don't need good reasons, though. The only reason at this moment is the reasoning of my nerve endings. Then comes screaming; it sounds miles distant but it's getting louder quickly, almost as though the screamer is being transported from her own time to mine, to the present. It's a girl screaming, Mindy, and I close my eyes...

...and open them to darkness and chaos, being pulled, pulled, my hand on the shivering steering wheel, my knuckles white. Mindy, Mindy is screaming, her hands shoved into her mouth, I can see her clearly in the dome light in the cab of the truck. Ah God, my knees, my nose, everything is pain, but worse than the pain is the fear. Mindy reaching out to me and the steering wheel shifts and my hand is pulled loose. I bounce roughly on the seat, my teeth taking off what feels like half my tongue, filling my mouth with a hot, salty flood. Then I am bouncing backward, I stare at Mindy, she is going away, the truck is going away, getting smaller as I go away. I twist, wrenching my back and I see over my shoulder to blueberry bushes, ghostly and shaking. I'm being dragged toward them and in them I see...

"A monster, a monster..." I am mumbling, rolling on my back in the sand. I sit up abruptly and they are all four staring at me, five if you include the horse. Deep shame slams into me and my face suffuses with blood. It's always like this, like being caught doing something nasty. My first thought is to tell them to go fuck themselves but I curb it. I know that at least half of my problem right now is the adrenalin, the fear that still bubbles, poisoning my mind even though I know–*I know*–I'm not in any immediate danger.

I lean forward and put my head in my hands. I take some deep breaths and will my heart to slow. A hand descends lightly upon my shoulder giving me a small start, but it's only

True…somehow I know this without opening my eyes.

"JD, are you all right?" she asks, nearly whispering. Her voice is threaded with warm concern. Amazingly, she doesn't yet ask me what I've 'seen'. For most people, it's the first thing they want to know.

I nod, my head in my hands, not wanting to look up just yet. I need to flush a little more of the fear from my system. Right now, what I saw is a big blur. It's as though I sometimes come out of these visions gripping a big bag of snakes, writhing and jumbled and potentially very dangerous. I have to keep calm and then I'll be able to sort and order the memory in a way that will be of the most help. But this vision was a bad one and it will be a few minutes before I can shake the terror.

"I'm right here," she says, and I feel her sit in the sand next to me, her shoulder pressing into mine. Her body absorbs some of the tremors shaking mine. It's an incredibly good feeling.

"Thanks," I say, my voice rough and quiet. "Thank you. That helps."

Tears burn into my eyes but I will them away, too. I know it's just the fear. I know that's all it is. *But* there is something about her nearness that touches me; I have to admit that to myself. Her stalwartness. The fact that she seems not at all freaked out by my…abilities.

My very first impression of her had been her beauty, my

second her pain, and now my third impression…is her strength.

I open my eyes and she is looking at me. Her eyes are fathomless, and she blinks slowly and smiles.

"Getting better?" she asks, but it is almost *not* a question, as though she has some small window into my inner workings and can see the distress receding.

I take a deep breath and what comes to me is her scent, clean and somehow earthy, and that chases the last bit of fear from me. I nod.

There is a familiar leather creak and then Trooper Stiles is in front of me, his hand held out. I let him pull me up and then I turn and pull True up next to me.

"Well?" Trooper Stiles says. He is looking at me intently. "I know you saw something…what was it?"

A scream rings through the woods, seeming to come from everywhere at once, ululating through the pines. Trooper Stiles' hand goes instinctively to his gun. Pepper prances nervously, shaking her head up and down and Roger puts a hand on her flank. His head swivels as he searches for the origin of the scream. I realize that True has grabbed my hand, and in her fear, she is squeezing it very hard. I look past Pepper. One of the twins is standing at the Jeep. His eyes are wide with shock, his mouth an unhinged black pit.

The other twin is gone.

-11-

Andrew struggles in Trooper Stiles' grip; Stiles is behind him with his arms around his chest. Roger is in front of Andrew, trying to reason with him, but he has to keep jumping aside so as not to get kicked.

"Let me go, dammit, you let me go, I have to find Jack…"

A flailing elbow catches Stiles in the stomach and he whoofs out a breath, bending over. But he doesn't turn Andrew loose.

"Andrew, listen! Listen to me! We *are* going to find him, I *promise* you. But you can't just go running into the woods. We have to do this methodically. We can't scatter all over; we're no help to him that way." Roger takes Andrew's face in his hands. "You *will* listen to me."

Andrew calms and at a nod from Roger, Stiles lets him go.

"True, you and JD wait here, but keep the Jeep running; we might need you in a hurry. Stiles, Andrew, we're going to fan out, no more than twenty feet apart, and search the woods to the east…that's the direction he went?"

Andrew nods and his face tightens.

"He just went to take a leak. That's all. He just had to pee."

Roger squeezes his shoulder.

"He's okay, I'm sure he's fine. We'll find him. Stay alert, okay? You too, Stiles."

I am surprised that Trooper Stiles is falling in line so quickly. I don't know how the balance of power works between the two state agencies, but I would have thought that State Troopers would have authority over Park Rangers. Maybe he's just bowing to Roger's superior knowledge of the woods. It strikes me as a remarkably cool-headed response on his part. Especially considering his firepower and obvious strength.

"I'll join your line," I say, stepping up next to Andrew. In my peripheral vision, I see his face swivel to me.

Roger shakes his head.

"Can't allow it, JD. No civilians," he says and starts away. "Let's go. Andrew on my left, Stiles, you're on my right."

I watch them start off into the underbrush. The Jeep revs to life behind me, and I go to lean against it. True is in the driver's seat, but she is turned sideways with her legs out the side, so she can face the direction they went. Her feet tap nervously on the running board.

"What could have happened?" I ask her.

"I don't know." Her features show the level of her perplexity. "Snake, maybe? The pine snakes can get to six feet or better and there are rattlesnakes out here, but…" she trails off, shaking her head.

"But he would have come hobbling back or at least still

be yelling if he'd been snake bit, right?"

She nods and her brows draw together in worry. Her dark eyes are on Roger and the others as they move deeper into the woods. I turn to look, too. It's hard to tell from this vantage point, but it seems as though Andrew might be a bit further in. His fear is making him reckless. Or at least, anxious.

I think that under normal circumstances, all three of them would have charged into the woods at the very beginning of the scream. But the oddness of the situation coupled with whatever I'd been saying and doing during my vision had put Roger's wind up. We are like rational people in a dark room made irrational by a stealthy, dragging footstep.

I shiver and shake my head to rid it of this imagery. I don't need to freak myself out any more; I'm freaked enough over the vision…what Gater went through.

"What was it you saw, JD? In your vision? You were mumbling something about a monster." It's almost as though she'd read my mind. An eerie unreality tries to cloud my brain. I look at her. Her chin is in her hands and her hair flows over her back like a dark wave. Her eyes staring into mine are filled with curiosity and concern, no judgment.

I turn and look back out to the woods.

"I was pulled from the pick-up, Gater was, I mean, but I was seeing everything from his viewpoint." I am cautious about how much I should say. I don't want to scare her and also, the visions are…they're sometimes untrustworthy.

Maybe it's not the visions themselves that are untrustworthy so much as that the view I'm given is skewed by the person's perception. Depending on the circumstances–especially those involving personal danger–perceptions can become alarmingly fluid.

"Do you feel everything he felt?"

"Yes, but only the physical," I say.

"What do you mean?"

"I mean that I don't feel his feelings, and I don't really think his thoughts. Sometimes, small bits of someone's thoughts come to me...but it's difficult to tell if that part is more intuition than vision."

"I don't understand."

"Well, when I'm seeing something from someone's perspective, I usually have some idea of what they're thinking, but that part of it isn't much different than studying someone's features and making a guess as to what they're thinking. Or maybe it's more like: if you know someone really well, have known them for years, you can usually guess what they're thinking, right?"

True nods. "Sometimes you don't even have to know someone for very long. Sometimes it's like you know someone the minute you meet him."

I turn and look at her again. She is looking right at me and her face is solemn, but there is the barest hint of a smile on her lips.

Yes. I know what she means. For sure, I know.

I look to the men in the woods. They're a good distance from us by now. If they haven't already found Jackson in that direction, then my guess is they're not going to. The scream was closer by.

"Some of the time it's more like watching TV...I see a person as they are at that moment in time. I can't read their minds or anything, but I can usually tell what they're thinking. I don't know if that's part of the process or straight intuition."

"Maybe it's too intertwined to be able to tell the difference?" she suggests.

I'm kind of amazed that she struck the nail so firmly on the head. I nod and look at her again. The vision of the terrified little girl flashes through my mind.

"Listen," I say, "I want to ask you about–"

There's a shout, and True and I turn the way the others had gone. Trooper Stiles, who'd been on Roger's right flank, is running toward Roger even as Roger is running to where Andrew had been.

My eyes sweep the woods, but I see no sign of Andrew. Had he fallen? Bent over to look at something? Where is he?

Stiles is making up the distance between him and Roger and now he passes him, crashing noisily through the underbrush. True jumps from the Jeep and drifts ten anxious feet closer to where the others are running, almost as though a weak magnetic force is at work in her. Her hands are balled into fists.

"He's drawn his gun," she says, her voice low, almost as if she's talking to herself.

I look past her and see that Stiles has indeed pulled his gun. He's stopped running and now turns in a tight circle just as Roger catches up to him. They confer, and then Roger turns in our direction, cupping his hands around his mouth.

"Did you see…" he yells and then I see him hitch in a deep breath, preparing to yell again. "…where he went?"

Sound travels oddly depending on the level of moisture in the air. On a really humid day like this, sound seems almost strained, as though held back by all those miniscule droplets of vapor–almost akin to shouting underwater.

Roger's voice reaches us, thinned and elongated, and then falls like a stone.

I shake my head slowly as True cups her hands to her mouth and shouts the answer: no.

Roger puts his hands on his hips. His exasperation is easy to read, even at this distance. He and Stiles confer again, and then start back toward us, Andrew-less.

True and I move a small way away from the Jeeps and stand at the edge of the sandy clearing. True's concern is evident in her posture and her anxiously drawn features. Her hands are on her hips and her jaw tightens and releases, tightens and releases.

Personally, I'm starting to be very afraid. Two people go missing almost as soon as we hit the woods? Are you kidding me? A large part of me wants to just run and run, preferably screaming, until I am out of these woods but looking at True steadies me…she's anxious, yeah, but she's not scared.

A hissing pop from behind me makes me jump and turn, my heart slamming up into my throat. Pepper, who'd been standing patiently next to the further Jeep, is snorting and backing away.

I voice my first, panicked thought, "Was that a snake?"

True is next to me, her shoulder against mine. She takes my hand.

"No," she says, her voice low. "Look at the tires…"

On the further Jeep, the one Andrew, Jackson, and Trooper Stiles had been riding in, both back tires were going flat.

Christine Dougherty

-12-

Roger has reached the clearing with Trooper Stiles at his side. Their uniforms are marked with large patches of sweat under their arms and at their waists and necklines. Roger is nearly panting with exertion and he doubles over and grabs his knees. Pepper knickers anxiously.

"S'okay, Pep," Roger says, still bent over. "Relax, girl."

"Where did Andrew go?" True asks. We're both momentarily distracted from the flattened Jeep tires.

Trooper Stiles is checking the contents of his belt, and when Roger doesn't offer an immediate answer, he does.

"We all heard something and it was closest to Andrew. He took off running so Roger and I started toward him…but…" he trails off, glancing at Roger.

Roger straightens, taking a deep breath and running his hand over his forehead.

"But he disappeared," Roger finished for Stiles. "There one second and gone the next. I don't know if I looked away or looked down for a second while I was running, but all I know is he was gone."

"Where? Where could he go?" Confused aggravation snaps bright red threads through True's voice.

"I don't know," Roger says and puts a hand on True's shoulder. "But I'm going to take Pepper and track him. I'll find him. He certainly can't have gone far."

True looks uncertainly in the direction they'd just come. It was vast, crowded, silent, sun-dappled forest as far as the eye could see.

"I'm coming with you," she says, but Roger is shaking his head before she even finishes.

"The Jeeps can't go into the woods…the trees are too close together. You'll be stopped before you get fifteen feet. Go back to the station. Phone Kathy and tell her we need everyone in. Get one of the quads and come back…it's only five miles or so…you'll be able to catch up to me. You take one Jeep and Trooper Stiles can drive the other–"

Roger had been in the process of gesturing toward the Trooper. He stopped abruptly when he saw Stiles squatting at the Jeep's rear tire.

"Is that a flat?" Roger started toward the Jeep. "How quickly can you get the spare on there? We'll need all the help…" he trailed off as his eyes happened on the other rear tire. His mouth fell open.

"They're both flat," I say, and he turns to me, his face radiating confused astonishment. "Both back tires on the Jeep. Flat."

"How? When did that…what happened here?" He's turned back to True and now Stiles is circling the Jeep. At first, I think he's inspecting the tires and then I realize he's looking at the sand around the Jeep. Smart. I hadn't thought

72

of that yet. But with everything happening so quickly, can you blame me?

"It just happened," True told him. "As you were coming back through the woods. JD and I had our backs to the Jeeps when we heard a popping, hissing noise. Turned back and the tires were going flat."

Stiles stands and crosses his arms over his chest.

"JD," he says, his eyes still on the ground. "What was it you saw? In your vision?"

I shift, uncomfortable.

"Why?" I ask. Fresh embarrassment colors my face. I am used to people nay-saying the visions...but it puts me eternally on the defensive about them.

But Trooper Stiles never even glances up. His eyes seem glued to the area around the Jeep.

"'Cause I don't know what made these tracks," he says and finally looks up at me. His face is set in serious lines and his eyes are hollow with concern. "But it wasn't a human."

Christine Dougherty

-13-

The trees flash by. I glance at True. Her hands are tight to the steering wheel. Her face is grim but calm. I look back to Trooper Stiles. He's holding his hat on with one hand, the other wrapped around the roll bar. True is pushing the limits of speed for this sandy trail and the Jeep is bouncing and sliding accordingly.

I face forward again. I am debating with myself on what to do once we get back to the Ranger Station. Could I offer to ride back out here again with True? I could ride behind her on the quad or maybe even drive one myself. Most of me is saying no way…once you're out, you're out…get back to the hospital and safety…they can take it from here. But still. Another part of me–a small part, it's true, but at least it's there–wants to stay and help.

I'll do it, I decide. I'll tell her I want to come back and–

There's a loud, booming crack like close thunder and suddenly the world seems to be all rushing green and black spikes. An enormous pine tree is falling right into the path of the speeding Jeep.

Trooper Stiles is yelling from the back seat. True's arms strain as the Jeep bounces inexorably toward the mass of fallen pine. The top of the tree has completely covered the width of the trail.

I brace myself for either impact or the roll. If True has to turn the Jeep at this speed, a flip is almost a guaranteed outcome. I remember that the Trooper hadn't belted himself in. No matter how big and strong his arms are, he won't be able to pin himself in a rolling Jeep.

True is nearly standing on the brake. Her face is a tight grimace of effort. The Jeep hits a rut and bounces violently; True and I nearly knock heads as her hair whips across my face. I close my eyes…

…*and open them in a small, dark, dirty kitchen. A baby sits in a high chair. The baby is dirty, too. There is a small pink barrette holding one forlorn sprout of dark hair on top of the baby's head. Her mouth is an open wound of despair as she cries. Food on the tray has hardened to a crust that she picks at with her small, clumsy fingers. I look down and there is a woman on the floor…either passed out or dead, I can't see which. I look at the baby again. Her cries have tapered off and she is sucking her fingers, and if I didn't know better, I'd swear she was looking right at me…*

My eyes pop open as the Jeep reconnects hard with the ground and then I feel the left side, the driver's side, start to rise. *This is it*, I think, *we're going over!*

Then it feels as though we've been caught in a giant's net…all at once, our forward momentum stops. I'm thrown against my belt, my neck snapping painfully. Trooper Stiles' head appears between True and I. Luckily, he'd caught himself with both arms on the seats–otherwise he might have been impaled on the stick shift.

The Jeep rocks gently. My eyes go from Stiles to True. Her hands are tight to the wheel, her arms locked straight. Her eyes are wide with amazement and her mouth hangs open.

I turn, my neck twanging painfully, and follow her gaze. The front of the Jeep has, at first glance, become a pine tree. The stubby snout is covered in green needles and bits of torn bark. I shift higher in my seat to see better and the Jeep rocks with my movement. What the hell?

My eyes adjust to what I'm seeing and I realize the Jeep has been impaled on a large branch. It sticks up through the Jeep's front hood like a pushy, muscular arm. It seems almost to point back the way we came, like a warning.

"Ho...ly...shit," the Trooper breathes next to me. His round-brimmed Trooper's hat has shifted to the back of his head. It makes him look like a bumpkin, countrified. He pushes himself back into his seat and then rights the hat on his head.

Then I look at True. Her body shakes with tremors.

I remembered the desperate, hungry baby in the vision I'd had when her hair touched my face. Had that baby been her? I thought so, yes.

"True?" I say, not sure what I want to ask her or to say. I just want that dazed look to leave her eyes. I want to stop the frightened tremors coursing through her body.

She turns to me.

She's laughing.

Her face is lit with an amazed gladness but hysteria also bites and snaps at the tone of her laugh. Then I can't help it, I'm laughing, too. True points at the tree sticking out of the engine compartment, then puts her hands to her stomach, closing her eyes and shrieking laughter into the pines above us.

I can't stop laughing. The Jeep rocks harder, and I think 'down will come JD…cradle and all' and that makes me laugh even more.

We had survived something that could have been very bad. One or all of us could have been thrown from the Jeep or impaled on that branch. We were so lucky.

It is so funny.

I become aware of a low rumble from the back seat and I look back to see Trooper Stiles, his hands over his mouth. His eyes are wide with shock, but his shoulders shake with mirth. It's as though he can't believe his own inappropriate reaction to what had just happened to us.

He is the first to stop.

He clears his throat and looks over the side of the Jeep. I look, too. We aren't far off the ground, about two feet, and the back tires aren't off the ground at all. The Jeep is not really unstable, just bouncing gently on the branch. I unbelt and hop out. I tilt the seat forward so Trooper Stiles can get out. The Jeep sways on its branch, but with the back tires firmly on the ground, it isn't in danger of tumbling.

"Looks like we'll have to go back for the other Jeep," Trooper Stiles says. He nods to True as she comes around to our side. The amusement still dances in her eyes.

"Let me get this spare off and then we'll roll it back with us."

She opens the tailgate and grabs the tire iron then starts on the lug nuts holding the spare to the tailgate. She moves competently and without any self-consciousness. In a way, I envy her. Then Trooper Stiles steps to her side and puts out his hand for the lug nuts. She turns to him with a warm smile and puts them in his open hand.

Now I envy him.

Why hadn't I thought to go and help her? Dummy, that's why. Big, damn dummy.

She pulls the spare from the Jeep. It's a full size spare with a metal rim and it's obviously heavy. It crashes to the ground at her feet, falling to its side. She bends to right it.

I stand with my hands behind my back, watching.

Trooper Stiles clears his throat and I glance at him. He rounds his eyes at me and then inclines his head to True as she struggles with the spare. His meaning is clear: help the girl.

It's like a slap on the ass and I jump forward and get my hands under the tire. Now True's warm smile comes my way.

"Thanks, JD," she says, and she starts back the way we'd come.

I look at Stiles again and this time he smiles and raises his eyebrows. See? He seems to be saying. Wasn't that easy?

"Don't say I never did you any favors," he says quietly and smiles.

I smile back and blush again. "Okay, I won't."

"Come on, guys…let's get a move on," True says from fifteen feet down the trail. "You don't want to be out here all night, do you?"

Surprisingly, my first thought is: that might not be so bad.

Shows how much I knew, huh?

-13-

We'd only gone a mile or two before the crash, so the walk back didn't take long. We didn't talk very much. Too hot, too tired, and in my case–too worried about the odd circumstances of being out here.

With all the activity, I hadn't had much time to reflect on everything that was going on. Most likely that was for the best, because now, as we walked and I had time to think, my mood was plummeting. Fear and despair were trying to pull a dark curtain in my mind.

I sensed that Stiles and True had caught a little of this gloomy mood, too.

The closer we got to where we'd left the other Jeep, the more tense I felt. There was no good reason for it, either, from anything I could see. The afternoon was getting late, but besides time rolling on, there was nothing that should have made me nervous. Or at least, more nervous than I have been from the start.

We come around the last little bend in the trail and now I can see the abandoned Jeep. It looks odd and I'm puzzling it out, trying to decide what looks wrong, when True shouts, "Andrew! Jackson!" She drops the tire and takes off running to the Jeep.

My unease is suddenly large in me, breaking over me like

a wave, shocking me with a cold certainty that something is about to go horribly awry. I want to call True back, warn her to go slowly, but she is already next to the Jeep.

She screams.

Her hands are fisted together at her chest and she takes a stumbling step back, almost falling. Stiles sprints to her side and steadies her. I reach them and look from True into the Jeep.

Andrew and Jackson are sitting in the seats–I don't know which twin is which, so I don't know who is in the driver's seat and who is in the passenger. But I don't think it matters. They are both dead, held in place by the seatbelts.

They are covered in blood, but it's hard to tell what, exactly, has killed them. Their eyes are open and staring at nothing and large horse flies buzz busily, lighting on the twins' red-soaked clothing.

The smell is overwhelming, tinny and salty and somehow *fresh*. I feel my gorge rise. I take a few steps back, trying to avert my eyes. Then I'm pushed roughly from behind. I almost tip forward right into the tub of the Jeep and only catch myself by pitching my weight to the left. I stumble onto one knee but am able to catch myself and scramble up.

Trooper Stiles is standing over me, his mouth pulled into a grimace.

"Touch them," he says, his voice a terrified growl. "You can touch them and–"

"What? No! No way!" In my sudden fury I actually take a step *toward* him and in his confusion he steps back. Then the weird anger/fear combination on his face clears and he is the affable Trooper once again.

"I'm...I'm sorry," he says, putting his hands out, palms up. "I was just, I thought maybe if you touched them, you could see..." Now his features are pulled down in desperation. "Christ, maybe you could see what did this to them."

I look at the twin corpses with fresh horror. Touch them? *Touch* them?

"He can't." It's True's voice, flat but not accusatory. "It might do something bad to him." Her eyes shift to me and then past me to the twins. Her face is very white and her lips tighten as tears spring to her eyes. "We have to find Roger; he can't have gotten very far," she says. "We can't let this happen to him, too."

I glance at the Trooper and realize he is thinking what I'm thinking. We have to make sure this doesn't happen to *us*, either.

"True, I don't know how we'll find him," Stiles says, leading her away from the Jeep. "He's got a half hour on us already. And he's on a horse."

"He won't be traveling fast. He thinks..." she shakes her head. "He thinks he can track them. He's got some kind of fascination with Native American lore and supposedly he's one sixteenth something or other, Pawnee or Cherokee or I don't know what…" Her voice is rising and she hitches in a breath as though to check herself and continues more calmly. "He's a very nice guy, but, well, you saw him! With that feather and…he just…he just thinks he's an Indian. Honestly, I could track better than him, and I for sure can track a horse."

True is standing in front of Trooper Stiles and I can see a jitter of impatience in her stance. But she is maintaining her cool, even in the face of the dead twins in the Jeep. My admiration for her shoots higher than even the tallest pines that surround us.

She continues. "I'd rather have you with me than not, but if you want to take JD and hike out, get some reinforcements, then that's what you should do. But I'm going after Roger." Her chin lifts, but it is not an obstinate gesture, just determined.

Trooper Stiles nods.

"Okay, I'm with you. We'll find Roger. But on one condition: we only search until about an hour before dark. That should give us time enough to get out while it's still daylight."

True nods. Then she turns to me.

"JD, you should hike out. It's not that far and it's just one trail…you won't get lost."

I'm already shaking my head.

"No way; I'm staying with you and Trooper Stiles. Safety in numbers, right?" I try to smile but the corpses behind me are a pretty effective mood dampener. The smile crawls across my face like a dying slug.

She nods and turns. At the very edge of the trail, where the woods begin, I hesitate. True and Stiles get about ten feet in before I force myself to leave the trail.

Now I am officially in the woods.

And I don't like it at all.

***

True's right, it is easy to track a horse in the Barrens. Even I might have been able to follow the trail set down by the horse's large body and plodding hooves–branches broken, blueberry leaves in a small pile where she'd brushed them from the bush, and of course, her hoofprints were deeply indented half moons in the sandy soil.

Sandy soil is one of the benchmarks of the Barrens. The soil is actually so full of sand that the ground looks pure white in patches. I can imagine how it would glow in moonlight, eerily translucent. That thought leads me to imagining the woods after dark. Creatures waking to rustle around, searching for sustenance. Frogs peeping from tree trunks. Countless insect life. Owls soaring in silence to pick off the little mammals–chipmunks, mice, maybe even a wayward squirrel. To me, it is a brutal scene, reeking of danger.

I have to stop thinking about it.

I look over at Trooper Stiles. His face is red with exertion and the heat. He *is* in full uniform…no wonder he's struggling. He lifts his hand and brushes it down the side of his face and I'm immediately reminded of my cell phone. That in turn reminds me of something else.

"Hey, True," I ask, "Why don't you have a walkie talkie to call back to the Ranger Station?"

She continues on, but glances back at me.

"I don't want to upset you…I know the woods aren't your thing." She smiles a small, sad smile and it takes the sting out of her words. She seems not at all judgmental about my fear, however irrational that fear might be. It reminds me that I wanted to ask her about what I'd seen–the little girl, the neglected baby–but I can't, not in front of the Trooper.

"I won't get upset," I tell her, in part maybe to convince myself.

She glances at me again and shrugs.

"The walkies don't work out here. Not walkies or cell phones or CB radios…well, wait; that's not a hundred percent accurate. They work on occasion. You might get a word or two, but the rest is static. It's almost like the signals, um, float."

"Float?" Stiles asks.

"Yeah, like, you can get a bit of signal here and then a bit over there…but never one good, strong signal. Never enough." She is still moving forward, scanning the ground and the bushes for signs of Pepper's passage. "It starts at about five miles in and by eight, you're done for. Some people say it's because of the base." Her last sentence was tossed out almost as an aside. Obviously she was taking it for granted that we all know what she meant by 'the base'.

I do know, actually. She means the Algonquin Air Force Base. It sits at the edge of the Barrens behind miles and miles of electrified fence. It draws a lot of speculation and rumor mongering. Dex has lots of connections there; I'm not sure why. Maybe just because he's a news guy.

"How do you communicate to do your jobs?" Stiles asks, and his voice is intensely perplexed. Like most twenty-first century Americans, he can't conceive of being 'out of touch'.

True shrugs again. She reaches out and deliberately bends a thin branch down. She'd been leaving 'marks' like this one all along the trail. Without them, she'd explained, we'd have trouble finding our way back to the Jeeps.

"The old fashioned way, I guess. You have a task to do, you go in and complete it, you come back out. And we rarely go in as a single. Most everything we do involves at least two people, and things like controlled burns involve everyone. We yell a lot and wave our arms around. I've only been at this station for a month, but that's the way it is at all the Ranger stations in the Barrens." She sighs, and I see a glimmer of unshed tears in her eyes before she turns away.

Trooper Stiles and I look at each other, and he raises his eyebrows at me and tips his head toward True. I know he's trying to communicate something to me, but I didn't know what. I shrug my shoulders at him and raise my hands palms up.

He nods toward True again and makes a shooing gesture.

Oh. I get it. I should go and walk next to her. Comfort her in some fashion.

You know what? It's a good idea. We could both use a little comfort, I guess.

So, how come I can't get my feet moving any faster?

I put my head down and jam my hands in my pockets and then am pushed roughly on the shoulder. Not hard enough to make me fall, but I do stumble forward a few steps and my hands go out to steady myself and I end up grazing True's shoulder.

I glance quickly back at Stiles even as True turns to me. Stiles has his hand over his mouth to hide a smile.

True's eyes are on mine and I open my mouth to speak.

"Hey!" The shout comes from ahead of us, making me jump and turn in that direction. "Hey, over here! I found something!"

It's Roger. He's about fifty yards away and Pepper is behind him. He is, indeed, waving his arms around.

"Oh, thank goodness," True murmurs and runs in Roger's direction.

I stare after her as waves of relief and despair flow through me. I should have said something. But I'm glad I didn't because it would most likely have been the wrong thing. Somehow, I still find myself wishing I'd said something.

A heavy hand is on my shoulder and I turn to Trooper Stiles' lopsided, commiserating smile.

"She's a nice person," he says.

I nod. I know that, I do. But it doesn't change the fact that I'm a sympathetic psychic who chooses to live full-time in a mental hospital. I mean, seriously, what am I supposed to do? Ask her to join me in crafts? Squire her to dinner in the ringing, moaning, crying cafeteria? Dinner by insanity—how romantic.

Stiles must see some of this in my expression, because he squeezes my shoulder.

"I'm not telling you to marry her, JD. Just talk to her."

I nod. Why am I so preoccupied with True?

At this point, I should be preoccupied with my own survival.

Christine Dougherty

-14-

"The twins are dead?" Roger's face is a study in incredulity. True nods, her lips compressed. I notice a slight hitch in her breath when she opens her mouth to speak; then she controls her emotions.

"Yes, both of them. I don't know who's out here with us Roger, but it's someone deadly."

Roger's face is stunned. He addresses Trooper Stiles.

"Could it have been an animal? Maybe even a mountain lion or a bear? They're rare in this area but not completely unheard of, I mean…"

The Trooper is shaking his head.

"No. In my opinion, from what we saw, they were executed in some fashion. The one in the driver's seat…" he glances at True, his face a question.

"Andrew," she supplies and the hitch is back, but she controls herself.

"Okay, Andrew was covered in blood, but there was none on the ground near him, none in the foot wells of the Jeep. Jackson had less blood on him, but there was still enough…whatever happened to them happened somewhere else and then they were placed in the Jeep after they'd died. I'd swear to it."

Roger takes a step back, his knees buckling, but luckily

Pepper is there for him to lean against. His hand goes to her mane in what looks like a completely unconscious gesture of comfort-seeking. Just like a little kid with a blanket or a special teddy bear.

Or the way you'd turn to a loved one.

Which makes sense.

"They're dead? You're sure?" Roger's voice is strained and it breaks across the last word.

True steps forward and puts a hand on his arm.

"We're sure, Roger," she says quietly. "There was no way to mistake it. You could tell from their…from their eyes. Whoever did it is sick but also very, very strong. It would take a lot of effort to get them in the Jeep seats that way. That's why we have to get out of here."

Roger shakes his head as if to try and clear it. His mouth is hanging open and his fingers are tangled in Pepper's mane as his hand opens and closes, opens and closes.

"I just can't believe it. I've worked with those boys for ten years; since they started as Rangers. I taught them everything I know and…" He swallows and looks at True. "I just can't believe it."

He looks older, as if the shock of the news of the twins' death had aged him ten years in ten minutes. He runs his free hand over his forehead and then, to my surprise, he looks at me.

"JD, do you know what happened to them? Were you able

to see it? Feel it?"

I shake my head and blush. My 'talent' has never struck me as more useless than it is right at this moment. It's hard to make people understand how random it is. I don't have any control over it, and it can also, at times, pose a threat to my personal safety.

Roger's hand untangles from Pepper's mane and he comes over to me.

"JD, you have to try and see who did that to Andrew and Jackson. I know that you didn't know them, but I *did*. I've known them for ten years now. They were good boys, JD. I know that you're scared out here but you have to…you have to find out what…"

I am still shaking my head. I cross my arms over my chest.

"I know you're scared." Roger's voice has a note of impatience. "But you have to help us. You have to—"

"JD, show him your ankles." True's voice is soft but very firm. I look to her, startled. How did she know?

She raises her eyebrows and nods.

"Show him," she says.

I look from True to Roger. Roger's face is drawn in lines of confusion. Trooper Stiles comes closer and stands next to Roger, looking at me with expectant concern.

Guess I might as well get this over with.

I sit and roll the heavy jean material up and over the tops

of my boots. The boots come to about mid-shin, so I have to unlace them and pull them off. My white socks have what at first look like red stripes around the ankle, but it's circlets of blood. I peel my socks down carefully, wincing. It's painful, yes, but certainly not the worst thing I've had happen.

My ankles are swollen, bruised and–there's no other word for it–they look chewed.

True kneels next to me.

"I knew you had something wrong, but I didn't think…" her voice trails away. She shakes her head, looking at the wounds. "I didn't know it was that bad." Now her eyes are on mine and the ache in my ankles becomes very far away…very secondary. I didn't know a beautiful girl could cure pain merely by looking at you. But it's not just her beauty that soothes, I realize; it's her compassion. Her intelligence. Her grace.

"How did you know?" I ask.

She shrugs and a small smile touches her lips.

"You looked as though you were walking across hot coals ever since you…saw whatever you saw when we first got here. It can be very dangerous for you, can't it? Your ability?"

I shrug but then nod. No false modesty here.

I pull my socks back up, rolling them carefully over the wounds. When we get out of here, I will most likely have to soak them off. The drying blood is going to fuse these socks to my ankles. I don't look forward to it. But like I said before, I've had worse.

I pull the boots on, lacing them tightly and wincing.

Trooper Stiles' hand appears in front of my face and he pulls me upright. Roger puts a hand on my shoulder.

"I had no idea. I'm sorry, son," he says. The black crow's feather in his hat glints in a patch of afternoon sun. "I'm just upset, you know, about the twins."

I shrug and nod. Trooper Stiles, Roger, and I stand awkwardly. At least, I know *I* feel awkward. Trooper Stiles reaches out and mauls my shoulder with his big hand.

"Listen, it'll be okay, all we have to do is—"

"Guys?" It's True. She's about fifteen feet away and turning in a slow circle. Her brows are drawn together and her hands rest on her hips. There's a line of tension in her posture that puts me on alert.

She glances back at us and her face is deeply troubled.

"Our tracks…all the marks I made…they're gone."

***

We walk in a haphazard single file line behind Roger on Pepper. True first, then me, and Trooper Stiles bringing up the rear. Nothing had been planned in our positions; we more or less fell into them. Except Roger, of course, being in the lead. Roger had decided on this direction, saying that the trail we'd driven in on was a main one and we'd cross back into it in a short time.

To me, it just feels like we are traveling deeper into the woods. But it's hard to tell for sure. Every direction looks the same–pines, pines, bushes and more pines. There's an occasional pin oak trying to add variety, but they are weak siblings compared to the tall conifers.

We haven't talked much. It's as though we're each holding our breath. There is also a feeling of being watched...even if it's just me that feels it in my heightened state of paranoia. I listen to the cicadas whine and buzz and it's such an insectile, foreign sound; I feel as though it's beginning to bore into my brain like tiny, alien drills. I need to distract myself. I trot up to walk next to True.

It's hard to walk side by side, the underbrush is just too dense.

"True, how could all the marks be gone? Wouldn't we have heard someone scouting along behind us?"

"I would have thought so, yes. But sometimes sound is funny out here, especially when it's this humid and still. If someone was very woods savvy, I guess they might have been able to tag along behind. It's not as though we were making any real effort to be quiet." Her voice is low and controlled. She glances at me and smiles. "Don't worry about that just yet, okay? We'll get back to the trail and get out of here, and then we'll try and get the rest of it figured out. One thing at a time, right?" She reaches for my hand and gives it a brief squeeze, and I smile and drop back behind her again.

When she had taken my hand this time, I'd had a brief flash, so fast and so distant it was like trying to watch your neighbor's television…through the curtains. I'd heard a little girl screaming. It wasn't the joyous scream of play, it was a scream riddled with pain and terror. Vague shapes, big and dark, moved in the vision, seemingly called by the screams. Or causing them.

I am thankful the vision was hazy and didn't last long. There's a lot of pain and suffering in True's past. It's hard to reconcile with this calm, brave, strong, competent woman walking ahead of me.

"Roger," True says, and her voice is still soft but abrupt as if she has just remembered something. "When you called to us, you said you'd found something. What was it?"

Roger turns in the saddle, his crow's feather dipping in time to Pepper's gentle walk. He glances from True to me to Stiles and then let his gaze rest back on True.

"I'll tell you…show you…when we get back to the trail."

He turns around just as Pepper makes a small leap over a downed tree. It's my turn to have my memory jogged.

"True, how unusual was it for that tree to have come down? It didn't look dead or anything…it was covered with green pine needles." With everything that had happened, I'd forgotten that one of my first impressions of that incident was that it seemed pretty coincidental the way that tree had fallen over just as we were trying to leave.

She glances back at me, troubled.

"Pines are shallow rooters for the most part, and in this sandy soil, well, you can see for yourself." She indicates the forest around us with a sweep of her arm. There are a lot of horizontal pines dotted throughout the landscape, but mostly they look like whittled sticks, barren of needles and in many cases, barren even of branches. "Their needles make them aerodynamic, that's why they aren't easily uprooted during wind storms, but…it *was* unusual, now that you mention it," she glances back at me again. "When we get back there, I'm going to take a look for what made it fall."

I nod but my first thought is: *if we get back there*.

Okay, I admit it, I'm a bit of a negative Nellie…hadn't you already come to that conclusion on your own?

We each seem lost in our own thoughts as we continue through the woods. I am startled by a small glow before me–directly before me. In fact, it's practically right under my nose–a lightning bug. I glance around as if waking from a dream. It's getting dark already. How did it get so late so fast?

I look back to Trooper Stiles. He is trudging stolidly along, head down. I drop back until we're even. He looks up and smiles.

"Doing okay, JD?" he asks.

I nod but then shrug my shoulders.

"It's getting dark," I say.

He looks around, seeming a little surprised. His eyes are shadowed beneath the brim of his Trooper's hat, but I can still read the unease in his expression. He looks at his watch and then ahead to True and Roger. They're a good thirty feet or so ahead of us. Pepper's dark brown coat is beginning to blend into the woods.

Yes, it's definitely getting darker.

"What time is it?" I ask Stiles, remembering he'd just checked his watch.

He shakes his head and looks at me with a smile that is meant, I am sure, to be reassuring. But I'm not reassured by the uneasy crease between his brows. Not at all, in fact.

"My watch has stopped," he says, and there's a strain in his voice from trying to keep his tone light. I think he has the same feeling of uneasiness that I have. I'm almost sure of it.

"I feel like we should have come across the trail by now," I say, and it's a relief to get the fear spoken and out, shared with someone.

He nods and looks at his watch again, an ingrained habit when time is mentioned to anyone who wears a watch on a regular basis.

"Let's get up there and talk to Roger, see if he thinks–"

He's cut off by a desperate, high-pitched scream. It is shrill and inhuman and I turn in time to see Roger pitched from Pepper's rising back. It is Pepper screaming as she stands, her front legs flailing desperately. True kneels by Roger and I see her struggling to hold him down.

Stiles and I sprint to them, our passage through the underbrush loud and chaotic, but still no match for the scene we're running toward.

Pepper is still screaming, striking out with her front legs, and as I watch, she jumps straight up and turns in mid-air, now kicking out with her strong back legs, her head lowered in determination.

We reach True and Roger, and Roger is struggling with her, trying to sit up. It is obvious that he wants to get to Pepper, but he has a large gash on his forehead that is cascading a steady stream of blood onto one side of his face.

Trooper Stiles joins True in holding Roger down and now their backs are turned to the desperately kicking Pepper. She has jumped several more times, a dark blur in the gloom, and I can see her kicks are already less robust. She's getting tired. I try and see past her, into the tangle of woods to see what it is that she fights.

There is a large shadow, indistinct but vaguely man-shaped, and it reaches for Pepper's legs each time she kicks out. Whatever it is, it too, seems to be getting tired.

"JD, come on!" It's True's voice behind me, she yells to be heard over the screaming Pepper. I look back, and she and Trooper Stiles are dragging Roger away from the stamping horse. Still he struggles, but his struggles have diminished.

He's losing a great deal of blood.

Pepper stops screaming, her breath rattling harshly through her lungs. Her sides are heaving and she is three shades darker, slicked with sweat. Now I hear another sound under Pepper's breathing and under the cracking of branches as Roger is pulled away...I hear a moan, and it raises every hair on my body.

It has an almost questioning quality, investigatory, as though it's trying to decide if Pepper has any more fight left in her. To my horror, I hear an answering moan from my left. I turn in that direction and though it's close to full dark, I can just make out a shape in a stand of Mountain Laurel, and I can see the pinpoint gleam of eyes set close together in a large head—the same eyes I'd seen back in my room.

The eyes that Gater saw as he and Mindy were attacked.

Now I know what happened to them.

Christine Dougherty

-15-

Trooper Stiles and True have managed to drag Roger behind a downed pine. I leap it and crouch next to them. Roger is still struggling, but he's weak and his eyes keep rolling back into his head. Concussion? Maybe. It's a good-sized bump he took to his head.

Stiles' face is set in lines of grim determination as he tries to keep Roger quiet and calm. He also keeps glancing back they way we'd come, and I see an alarming flash of fear in his eyes. Alarming to me, anyway. I don't want this big cop to be afraid of anything out here. If he's afraid, where the heck does that leave me?

True strips Roger of his uniform button-down leaving him in a T-shirt. She cuts a thick swath of cloth from the button-down with a small knife she produced from her pocket. She cuts another, thicker piece of cloth and folds it into a rough square. She takes the square of cloth and ties it in place over the cut in Roger's forehead with the thinner strip. She works quickly and efficiently. She does not glance in the direction we'd come. I don't know if this is because she is unconcerned or unaware.

The sounds of a fray still come to us from where Pepper stands her ground, possibly saving all our lives. Barely, just barely, I can hear the moans of whatever those creatures are.

"JD, what were they?"

My eyes snap back to True, and she is pulling Roger upright and then leaning him back against the tree. She glances at me.

"What were they?" she asks. "Bears of some kind? I couldn't see them very well."

"Those were *not* bears," Trooper Stiles chimes in. He was looking over the downed pine, squinting into the gloom. "I don't know what they were, but they were big. Bigger than a man. Bigger than me."

There's an odd tone in his voice. Awed and fearful, as if the thought of a creature bigger than him had blown his mind. I could see that the panic was trying to get a toehold in his thoughts. I know all about that, believe me. I also knew I had to put the brakes on any useless, circular thinking he was getting ready to bury himself with.

"Trooper Stiles?" I say.

"Trooper?" I say it again.

He doesn't respond, but True glances from me to the Trooper. I try again.

"Uh…Raymond? Ray? Do you see something out there?"

He glances at me and I can see the panic snapping and glinting in his eyes. Then they seem to clear as he focuses on me, on what I'm asking him.

"I don't see anything; I can barely see the horse." He glances out into the dark and then back to me. "I'm really sorry I got you into this. I'll get you out. You and Roger, too," he finishes, glancing at True.

Taking responsibility seems to have a galvanizing affect on him. It obviously clears his mind and sets him on the right track. He turns, putting his back to the log. Now we are in a rough semi-circle around Roger.

"True, I want you and JD to stay here with Roger." I hadn't noticed before–he's holding his gun. Now he fumbles around at his belt and I hear a distinct snap. "You keep this. It's high powered enough to stop a man, it should at least give pause to whatever is out there." He hands an ugly, black square of plastic to True. A taser. From the size of it, it was, indeed, a powerful one. "Turn it on here, but then stay clear of the points. This is a direct contact taser, not the kind that throws barbs. Use it if your assailant is near enough to reach. But make sure you aren't in physical contact with him or you'll get a similar hit." He reaches into his belt again and brings out a thin, short stick and hands it to me. "This is the only other thing I have. It's a telescoping baton. You can do some damage with it, but it's really only meant to subdue, you got me?"

I nod and pull on the point, drawing it out a few inches. It is also black and gleams wickedly in the dying light. I could imagine the sharp sound it would make as it sliced through the air. But I didn't have a lot of confidence in it. On bare skin, it might leave a good welt, but on fur? I don't know how much it would even subdue a furred creature.

Those things–whatever they were–certainly *looked* furry.

Something is crashing through the brush on the other side of the tree. Something big by the sound. Before we can even react to the noise, a large shape is leaping over us from the direction where Pepper had been engaged in combat. True throws herself forward over Roger, shielding him. Trooper Stiles rolls himself forward away from the log and pushes me over backwards, his arm heavy against my chest. I am the only one who sees Pepper as she leaps across us, screaming, blotting out the sky. Something patters wetly onto my face and into my eyes and I realize almost immediately that it's blood. It falls like a brief, hot rain and then she's over us and crashing away through the bushes on the other side.

The forest becomes deathly silent.

Then I hear another moan, somewhere out ahead of us. Then comes an answering chuff, closer and on our left and another moan off to our right. Stiles scrambles to his knees, looking back over the log, squinting into the gloom. True crouches protectively by Roger, her face a white disk. Every hair on my body stands at attention and I shiver wickedly.

Whatever is out there is circling us.

And coming closer.

A small vibration against my thigh is followed a split second later by a loud, burring ring. True and Stiles turn to me, wide-eyed in their shock and I'm sure my own face is a mirror to theirs. I freeze in my panic.

Stiles nods toward my pocket on the second ring.

"Answer before they hear it!" he says.

His admonition gets my limbs unlocked and I scramble up and sit with my back against the log. I fumble my hand into my pocket and pull out the vibrating, ringing cell phone. Free of the heavy denim of my jeans, it's instantly twice as loud. The screen glows in the semi-dark…the words 'Dex Hammond' appear in the display.

A furious screech from the other side of the log causes me to jerk and I fumble the phone, nearly dropping it. There is an answering screech on our right, followed by something big crashing through the brush. I am too disoriented to know if it's coming closer or going away. I almost scream in reaction, but then True's hand is under mine, steadying me. I slide a shaking thumb across the bottom of the screen, unlocking it and answering the call.

I hold my breath and listen to the night. I can hear Dex faintly and I lower the phone. There are no other sounds. True is looking past me into to the forest and Stiles still kneels at the log, but now his head swivels toward us. He raises and drops his shoulders. Then we hear a hesitant peep. Then another. Then a third a bit further away. The tree frogs are singing again.

I raise the phone to my ear.

"Dex?"

"JD, what the hell? Why didn't you answer me at first? You don't have your phone in the common room, do you? Don't take it in there, JD, you know Nora doesn't want the–" his voice stops abruptly. "JD, are you…are you outside? Is that tree frogs I'm hearing?"

I nod and then realize my mistake and I shake my head, trying to clear the layers of fog that panic seems to have stuffed in there.

"Dex, I'm in the Pine Barrens with–"

"What?" His tone is one of utter incredulity. "I don't think I heard you right, JD, did you say–"

"You heard me, I'm in the woods, in the Pine Barrens, ask Nora about it. I came out to help with finding some missing kids but, Dex, we're in–"

"You couldn't even go canoeing with me that one time! How come you…"

He is as frustrating as any real parent could ever have been.

"Dex, listen, we're in trouble out here. There's something out here with us…it's already killed two people and, I guess, one horse." Instinctively, I look in the direction Pepper had been running. "Or maybe not a horse, I don't know, but it did kill two Park Rangers. Dex, we're really in trouble. Roger–another Ranger–he's got a bad cut on his head, maybe a concussion but we're lost back here, and–" Hearing myself say 'lost', I choke up a little. It's my worst nightmare realized.

Dex must hear it in my tone. He reverts instantly to the calm and competent field reporter he'd once been.

"Hang in there, JD, I'll find a way to get you out. Are there any landmarks? Anything specific?"

I look around. "No. Just trees."

"Okay, listen carefully...do you have a—"

I look down.

The display reads 'call ended'.

The call just dropped.

I hit the button to redial the last call and I wait. Nothing. Nothing happens. I look at the display. No bars.

"Oh, shit."

"What is it? What happened?" Stiles asks, nearly crashing into me as he tries to see the display.

"The call cut off. He said 'do you have a' and then that was it. He was gone."

"Did you try and call back?"

I nod and then look at him.

"No bars."

"But the call just came in! How could that be?"

"It's like I told you earlier," True says. She's shaking Roger's shoulder. "Signals float out here." She looks at us and her eyes have an almost eerie glow in the half-light. "Whatever those things were, the phone scared them away. I think I saw a cabin on our way here. Let's get Roger up and back-track a little. I think I can find it. We need to regroup and give ourselves a minute to think. JD, keep your phone handy. He'll try and call back. Be ready to answer if the call gets through again. Okay, let's go."

She bends to Roger as Stiles and I look at each other, dumbfounded.

"Guys, come on," True says, her tone laced with the slightest bit of irritation. "Snap out of it. Stiles, help me."

Trooper Stiles holsters his gun and bends to help with Roger. I grip my phone, checking it compulsively. Ring, I think at it, ring, ring…but nothing happens.

I wish I could transmit as well as receive.

***

True and Stiles lay Roger down on a bunk built into the wall. Roger was in and out during our trek to the cabin, now he is mostly out again. The stain on the wad of cloth on his forehead hasn't gotten any worse, so at least his head seems to have stopped bleeding.

I look around the cabin. It's essentially one big, open room with a curtained off area on the side where there are two rudimentary beds. The furniture–a table, four chairs, and something that looks like it's supposed to be a couch–are made of rough-hewn pine and there are even areas of bark on the chair and table legs. It looks like someone hacked this entire cabin right out of the forest.

It's not big, maybe twenty feet by fifteen or so. There's a row of kitchen cabinets–shelves really–across a back wall. They're open with no doors, but there are some chipped dishes and a couple of frying pans. There's no stove, no refrigerator, no electricity, and (Stiles checked) no generator. Also–to my mortification–no bathroom.

It's a basic hunting cabin. That's what True said.

She stands back from Roger's bed and pulls the curtain to shield him from the light thrown by the lantern on the table. Then she puts her hands to the small of her back and stretches, eyes closed. The lantern light seems to catch and glint in the waves and spirals of the cascade of her black hair. She turns to us and smiles.

"I think he's going to be okay," she says and pulls out a chair. "He seems more tired than anything else. Might be in shock, too. We'll have to keep a close eye on him."

"How are we going to get him out of here?" Stiles asks.

True shrugs. "I'm sure he'll be better by morning."

Morning? My heart sinks. I think Stiles' does a little, too, because he echoes my thoughts.

"Morning?" His voice holds a tone of incredulity. "You mean stay here all night?"

"I don't know what else to do. Do you?"

He opens his mouth to answer and then closes it again, blinking. "No, I don't. I'm not sure staying here is such a good idea either, though. This place is not exactly Fort Knox, you know." He gestures to one of the 'windows'–a rough square covered in what looks like some kind of heavy waxed paper. It looks flimsy enough for a baby to crawl through.

True nods. "Yeah, I know. But we can't hike out. Who knows how far those things went or even if they went at all. They were quiet enough to follow us the whole way without being detected. They could be right outside that door."

I look at the door and my stomach drops. Those things could be right out there! Listening in even…do they understand us? Oh, man, this is really freaking me out.

True's hand is on mine and I jump. "It's okay, JD, I don't really think they're out there, I just meant that they're so–"

…quiet, be QUIET, Jesus just shut the hell up Christ I never heard such a crying CRYbaby in my LIFE what the hell is WRONG with you?" A woman with dark, bushy hair is standing over a toddler, a little girl maybe three or four years old with black curls and a ragged blue dress that used to belong to someone else a cousin maybe or just a friend of the family. Her little knees are scraped raw and the blood has soaked into her ankle socks. Her cheeks are red and chapped and tears course down her cheeks. She has raised her arms to the woman, "mama, mama" she cries, her little fingers kneading the air frantically. The woman rears back and brings her left arm up, way up, she is almost turned around under the curled spring that is her arm. Then she lets fly and strikes the baby across the face, open handed, sending the

girl crashing down onto the floor where she curls into a ball, crying harder, sobbing herself into hyperventilating. "God DAMMIT, Trudy, quit crying for God's sake you're giving me a headache...

I open my eyes, my hand on my cheek. True's eyes are filled with concern.

"JD, what is it, are you all right?"

I nod, my hand still covering my cheek and she peels it away and gasps. "JD, your face! It's red as a beet! What happened? Is this from...did you have a vision? Is that what happened? A vision did this to you?"

I nod again, unable to speak. I know for sure that True was that little girl. I can't imagine what it must have been like. What I just saw...it makes my heart quite literally ache in my chest. It aches for True.

Trooper Stiles leans closer to me, inspecting my face. "You're going to have a black eye, JD. What did you see? Was it something about those things that were chasing us?"

I want to deflect this line of questioning and move past it as quickly as possible. I shake my head.

"What were those things anyhow? True? Have you ever seen anything like that before?"

She waits a long time to answer, staring me directly in the eyes. I think she knows that I am trying to turn them away from the injury I just received. She looks at me consideringly and then nods the slightest bit. Her nod says: *I'll go along...for now.*

"No, but I didn't get a very good look," she says.

"You know what they could be, don't you?" Stiles says, leaning his elbows on the table. He still has his Trooper hat on and his eyes are shadowed under the wide brim. His breath agitates the small lantern flame and shadows dance devilishly across his features as though to help illustrate his vague words.

True crosses her arms over her stomach and sits back, a small hiss of disgust escapes between her lips. "Jersey Devil? Is that what you're saying? Trooper, there is no such thing."

Now Stiles sits back, too, crossing his arms over his chest. I felt like I should do the same, make it three for three, but I don't. I've heard about the Jersey Devil, of course. Anyone with any ties to Jersey has heard the story of poor old Mrs. Leeds and her unlucky changeling. The little mutant monster that had been chained in a crawlspace under their...

"...cabin." Stiles is saying, but I missed the first part.

"Come again?"

"'This could be the very cabin,' I was saying, the one where he was born. The little Leeds Devil."

"You don't really believe that; you can't! That Leeds story took place in...what? The twenties? Or thirties? You really think this cabin has been around that long? It would be dust by now. It would be termite food."

Stiles is shaking his head. "You don't know that. You

can't know! This cabin could be…I don't know…enchanted or something."

True frowns at Stiles and I have to admit: I do, too. 'Enchanted?' Did he really just say that? I think we have a closet Tolkien reader on our hands, folks. Who'd've thought?

He tightens his arms, embarrassed color coming up in his cheeks. "Okay, maybe not, maybe not," he leans forward again, his face earnest, "…but it could be where the stories come from."

"No. It's just a hunting cabin," True says.

She stands abruptly and goes to the sink at the back of the cabin. There's a hand pump and a pitcher half-filled with dusty water to prime it. There are three more jugs of water on the floor, left by the hunters who use this cabin twice a year; we'll have to be sure to refill anything we empty so the next people can get water, too. The pump groans and a glut of rusty water jets out and then as True pumps, it runs clear. She fills the pitcher and sets it aside then grabs three large plastic 7-Eleven cups from the open shelves. She fills each and then brings them to the table.

The water tastes rusty but drinkable. True drinks half hers and then grabs a rag from another open cabinet and dips it into her cup, soaking it.

"Here, JD," she says, scooting her chair closer to mine. Now we're knee to knee and she reaches across with the rag and begins to wipe at my face. "I'm tired of looking at the blood on you."

Blood? Oh, yeah, now I remember. It's from when Pepper jumped over us. I'd forgotten all about it.

True is very careful on the side of my face that got 'slapped,' moving the cloth in gentle circles. She looks into my eyes. I feel something pass between us, but I don't know what it is. Then she smiles as if *she* knows. I feel hypnotized by the darkness of her eyes. She's so beautiful. She leans a little closer and for a split second, I see Mindy from my earlier vision, leaning in for a kiss. Is True leaning in for a kiss? A kiss from *me*?

Stiles coughs into his hand, an obvious 'ahem' kind of sound, and True pulls back sharply. Now it's her turn to grow a bit of color in her cheeks. It looks good on her...really good.

"Well, listen," Stiles says and stands to stretch. "I think I'm going to take the other bunk. You two take first watch and then–"

A branch breaks and it sounds like it comes from right outside the door. Just like True said: they must have been there the whole time. Our goose is cooked.

True leans over and blows out the lantern and with her next breath, she's up and across the cabin, lithe as a cat and just as silent.

Stiles is still standing and now he has his gun drawn again. It glints dully in the little bit of moonlight that makes it first through the trees and then through the scummy paper on the windows. His eyes are fixed on True. She's a black silhouette against the slightly less black door.

Another branch snaps and then there's a low snorting sound…almost one of surprise. It doesn't sound like the creatures we heard earlier, but Stiles has trained his gun on the door. True looks back at him and raises her shoulders: what do you want me to do?

Stiles' chin lifts and he gestures for her to open the cabin door.

He will shoot the monster on the other side.

It will be taken completely by surprise.

An uneasy flutter brushes my insides. *Just adrenalin,* I think, dismissing the feeling. *That's all it is.*

The snort comes again and True's hand is on the rope that serves as a doorknob. She grasps it, getting a good strong grip and then she looks back to Stiles.

Stiles' eyes glitter menacingly and the fluttering in my stomach turns into a burning sensation deeper in my gut. *Adrenalin,* I think, *it's just adrenalin.*

Stiles holds up three fingers. He nods and True nods back: *on three.* Stiles mouths 'one' and nods. He mouths 'two' andTrue's hand grips tighter on the rope.

I have the sudden and inexplicable urge to launch myself at Stiles.

True starts to pull the door open as Stiles says 'three' and in that instant, I remember what that hesitant, blowing noise is and now I *do* launch myself at Stiles, hands up in an attempt to push his gun aside. Luckily for me, I fall short and crash onto the cabin floor; otherwise, I might have deflected the bullet right into True.

Stiles points the gun straight up without discharging it, turning at my sudden and alarming–though fruitless–attack. True had flung the door open and then turned at my movement, her hands going to her mouth to stifle a scream. Now she looks instinctively back to the yawning, defenseless door. A monster stands in the doorway, nearly blocking it and now True does scream. It's a banshee wail in the dark cabin and the monster in the doorway throws it's head back and snorts.

Behind me, Roger says, "Pepper!" making Stiles jump and turn in his direction, raising his gun.

I'm glad I'm already on the floor.

Because this is where I might have ended up, anyway.

***

Is it possible to feel jealous of a horse?

True runs the cloth over each of Pepper's legs, trying to clear away the spots of dried blood. She pats Pepper and murmurs gentle encouragement, calming the little horse. Yes, it's the same cloth she'd used on my face. Yes, it's the same tone of voice. I don't know whether to laugh or cry.

Roger laid back down after we got Pepper into the cabin and situated. He said he felt okay, just a little dizzy, but True had insisted he go back to the cot. Then she started ministering to Pepper. That's when I fell into the background.

True has Pepper in the 'living room' portion of the cabin and it seems a lot smaller with a horse in here. Trooper Stiles and I have resumed our spots at the little kitchen table, and we watch True as she works on Pepper.

Stiles must see some of the consternation in my face.

"Girls and horses," he says, his voice quiet. "What can you do? That's a bond that seems almost as old as time. Like us with dogs, you know?" He smiles at me.

I half smile back. I don't tell him that I actually prefer cats. Dogs are okay, too, but I like how cats keep to themselves, the neat, compactness of their lives. I respect that.

I am starting to dislike horses, though.

"I think I'm going to rack out," Stiles says, standing. He looks even bigger in the flickering lantern light. He addresses True. "Take it easy, but keep an ear out, okay? I bet Pepper is going to be a good early warning system. She seemed to know those things were there before we did."

True nods and hugs Pepper around the neck. "Yeah, you're a good girl, aren't you Pepper? Aren't you a sweetie?"

Stupid horse.

Stiles sees it in my face and claps me on the shoulder, smiling. "Take it easy, JD. Wake me up if you feel yourself falling asleep. When the adrenalin wears off, it can knock you out quick. And try not to worry too much; we'll be out of these woods before nine tomorrow morning, I'm sure of it."

I nod, but strangely enough, the events of the afternoon are losing their power over me, even if I don't understand why. How can I be in the middle of the Pine Barrens, chased by who knows what, hiding out in a run down cabin with two rangers, a trooper…and a horse…and not feel odd? I don't know how, but the truth is, I don't.

Listen, I'm a recluse, and that's the truth. I do my best to never leave my room, much less the hospital. Much less the hospital grounds. The last time I'd even been in a car was about nine years ago when I was sixteen. For Aunt Mayella's funeral.

But I don't want to think about that right now.

I stand and stretch, and I guess I groaned a little (okay, I know I groaned…I'm trying to get her attention back; can you blame me?) because True turns to smile at me.

"You okay?" she says. She gives Pepper one last pat on the shoulder and then comes back to the table. She pushes out the chair next to her. "Sit?" she says, and pats the seat of the chair.

"I think I'm going to stand for a minute or two. Wake up a little," I say, and I regret it instantly. Where do I think I'm going to go? Outside with the monsters? Over in the living room with the horse? True is still smiling up at me. I smile back, almost–*almost*–against my will.

"I wish I could ask if you wanted a Coke from the fridge, but…" I shrug my shoulders. "Looks like I'm tapped out."

She nods and smiles wider. "I could make you an omelet if we had some eggs. And a frying pan. And a stove," she says.

My smile widens. "Omelet sounds good. Maybe a cheese and mushroom one? If we had cheese, I mean, and mush-rooms."

"I could do that," she says. "If we had those things. I guess you'll just have to settle for rusty water and my com-pany." She indicates the chair again. Truth is, I'm starting to feel like a dummy standing here.

I sit.

"So. You really like horses, huh?" It is a sparkling con-versational gambit. I'm not sure why sitting has made me a little more nervous than I was before. Proximity? Yes, that's probably it.

She looks to where Pepper stands, head down, one back foot cocked and resting on the very tip of her hoof. Pepper looks worn out. So does True. So, most likely, do we all.

"Yes," True says in answer to my question but then says no more. My unease increases. True's head is down and her lips are slightly pursed, as though is considering something. I sit quietly, waiting for the result of her interior debate. Then she looks up.

Her eyes are deep and deeply within them, the lantern's flame is reflected and it dances sinuously. True's hair catches each flick and flitter of light and the shadows on her face are deep and mysterious. She looks like a Gypsy about to tell me my fortune.

"What do you know," she asks, "about me?" Her head tilts and it serves to throw a shadow over her eyes. Her tone is even, but I sensed a thread of something in her question...sadness? I think sadness, yes. "What did you see?"

I feel almost embarrassed, but I shouldn't. I can't help what I do. I don't have any kind of control over it. I hope she understands and isn't angry.

"I saw you, True. The first was you hiding; I think you were maybe five? It's hard for me to tell, but you were hiding from someone you thought of as a monster...that's what you were thinking, and you were afraid. The second time was you in a high chair, a little baby...I couldn't even begin to guess your age, I don't know very much about babies, but you were hungry and crying and someone was...on the floor? Passed out or dead, I can't know that part, either. The third time was..." I stop, noticing the tears falling in twin tracks down her cheeks. "I'm sorry." I put my hands together on the table, feeling deeply ashamed. I've made her feel terrible.

Then she puts a hand on mine. "It's okay; I'm okay. Please go on."

She has leaned in and now I can see her eyes again. She's

not angry or ashamed, only waiting to hear the rest.

"The third time, a woman hit you. You were crying. I think you were three or four and you had hurt yourself. You were reaching up for your...mom? I guess she was?...but she hit you and knocked you down." I sigh. "You had a very rough time. When did it stop? The abuse?"

She smiles a very sad smile. "Not for a long time. It was like that until I moved out when I was fifteen."

"Fifteen? Where did you go?"

"I went to a shelter first. I stayed there for a few months and the woman who ran it, Lisa, she and I got very close. She explained a lot to me that no one had ever bothered to explain, about abuse and alcoholism–my mom was an alcoholic. And she helped me understand it wasn't me, that it wasn't my fault. But even then, I was still too young to understand everything she was trying to tell me." She leans back and she is in shadow again. "I was a really angry kid, for a really long time." Her next question sends a shiver down my back, mostly because her voice takes on a tone of–almost harsh–interrogation. "You didn't see anything else? From when I was older?" Whatever she's thinking of is something she desperately does not want me to know. I'm glad I can answer her honestly.

"No, only those three times, and you were a little kid in two of them, and in the other one, you were just a baby..." Something snags in my memory and I sit up sharply.

"What is it, JD? Did you hear something outside?"

"No; no, nothing like that. It's just that in the one vision, the one where you were in your highchair...you...I could swear this happened...you *looked* at me. As if I was there in the room with you." I think for a minute. "True, where was your dad?"

It's the jackpot question–if the jackpot was, you know, tears and grief.

True lays her head in her arms and her shoulders are shaking. Oh, crap, now what? But I know now what. I pull my chair over next to hers and wrap my arm around her and she turns and folds herself into my shoulder. I let my body absorb the tremors shaking hers. There's nothing even remotely sexual about this; it's beyond that. I feel like I've known True for years with that deep and abiding understanding friends can develop if they are very good to, and careful with, each other.

The depth of her pain is stunning but even more stunning is the depth of her strength. She is a strong, functioning woman who has gotten past her past and moves through the world doing much more good than harm. And I admire her.

She sniffs and sits up, smiling a little. She considers the really dirty horse rag sitting on the table between us and grimaces and then wipes her face on her sleeve. That gets about fifty percent of her face cleaned up. Smiling, I offer her my arm and she laughs and then, holding my arm steady, she wipes her face across it. Then she laughs again.

"You know, I think that's just about the nicest thing any-one's ever done for me," she says.

I smile back but don't say anything. And then I change the subject.

I don't want her to recall that I'm also the one who caused her to remember her grief.

-16-

Pepper blows softly in her sleep. Her head is down and her eyes are closed, so she must be dreaming. Dreaming about the monsters she fought with? Or dreaming about being back in her warm, safe stable? I know which one I'd be dreaming about.

True and I are on the couch. That's why I have such a close up view of the horse. Her head is hanging over my knees. I know I was jealous of her earlier, but I am starting to appreciate her, now. Especially the reassuring heat she generates.

True is asleep. It's weird that I am the only one awake, the only thing standing guard between our crew and the danger that lurks outside. I would not have cast myself in the role of protector. This is a new feeling for me. Not sure if I like it or not.

I look up to the window covered in the yellowy, scummy oilcloth or plastic or whatever it is. It is glowing dully. The sun must be coming up. It gives me a wash a relief but then again, I wonder if it's childish to feel like those things out there will disappear obediently as the sun shows up. I don't know. I don't know enough about monsters. Not the kind out in the woods, anyway.

I wish we'd gotten a better look at them. Neither in real

life nor in the visions was I able to see them clearly. I know their heads–foreheads especially–seem misshapen. There's the hint of protrusion above their eyes, which are small and close set. Their shoulders seem shrunken but they must have a good amount of strength, they tussled with a horse and tossed around a truck, after all.

I look at Pepper, considering. *She* saw them. She got the clearest view of any of us. I wonder...

I reach my hand out and place it on her shoulder. I've never touched a horse before and am surprised by the solidity. She seems made entirely of some heavy, dense, but yielding rubber. And her fur? hair? is soft and coarse at the same time. Her back foot lifts and drops in her sleep and I feel a corresponding heaviness in my foot. It seems to be changing, becoming heavier and hardening and I glance down and see...

...it has become a hoof, and I have a weight on my back, but it's not too heavy it is actually almost a comfort. I see trees and bushes and I really want to stop at each bush and pull the sweet berries from them but there is a sense of urgency, of fear almost, from the being on my back. I can sense the agitation and discomfort of the beings behind me, too. They are my band, my family, and their anxiety becomes my own. I have to keep watch for them as they are keeping watch for me. We all keep watch. We sense the danger that lurks, the strange smell, the odd tickings and clickings from all

sides. I know they must be as aware of it as I am. That's why we are all afraid. Afraid of what is following. The things that are not known…

I pull my hand free of Pepper's side–yank it away, really–and shake my head. True is roused by my movement.

"You okay?" she asks, her voice muzzy with so little sleep.

"Yeah, I'm okay," I tell her. "Everything is fine; it's almost morning."

She stands, stretches, pats Pepper, smiles at me and then goes to the pump in the kitchen.

I look after her for a minute and then back to Pepper. It was weird, seeing through her eyes, feeling what she felt. Her all-encompassing desire to protect and be protected by her family. I'm not sure if I liked it. It felt as though I was giving up a lot–a lot of myself and also a lot of the sense of a singular 'I'. I've never had a family…maybe that's the way it feels.

Once again, I realize I'm a little jealous of Pepper.

I gotta get back to the hospital.

This field trip is doing weird things to me.

I stand, getting ready to shuffle past Pepper and join True in the kitchen, when Pepper's head comes up with a jerk. I stumble, the backs of my knees hitting the couch, and I fall back to where I'd been sitting a second before. Pepper blows and stamps her front hoof in an agitated way, her head swinging toward the door of the cabin. She's heard something we can't hear yet.

I look past Pepper to True. She's coming back toward us, alarm and concern lighting her features. There's a muffled thump on the cabin door and it shakes in its frame. True jumps back as the curtain to the bedroom area is pushed aside and Trooper Stiles is already fumbling the gun from its place on his belt. Roger is behind Stiles, sitting up in the bunk looking groggy and disoriented. The bandage on his head has shifted and a little of the ragged skin is showing. At least the bleeding has stopped.

I can't believe I'm noticing Roger's head when my own life might be in danger. Maybe some of Pepper's familial concern has rubbed off on me. Or maybe I'm just too scared to think straight. Yep, I think that's it; that's the one I'm going with.

There's another thump on the door; this one is harder. The door rattles again, showing wan morning light through the seams. I thought they would be gone at daylight. I don't know why I thought it, I just did. Too many vampires in the media lately, I guess. You just naturally start to assume that any monster is a vampire.

True's hands are curled over each other and she looks from the door to Stiles. With his free hand, he motions for her to come to him. Then he puts a hand toward me, palm up: *stay there.*

No problem. I stand and huddle closer to Pepper.

Trooper Stiles goes to the door and puts his head against the crack, listening. He's brave. I wouldn't put my head there. What if one of those things sticks something sharp in his ear? The thought causes me to put my hands over my ears and Pepper's eye rolls toward me like: *what are you, an idiot?* I put my hands back down.

Stiles' hand is on the rope pull and I shuffle back a few steps even as I notice True puts herself in front of Roger and pulls the curtain over them, leaving just her eyes to peek out. I know she does this involuntarily but she looks so much like a kid playing hide and seek that I almost smile. Then, Stiles opens the door.

The first thing I register is two big blood and gore spots about halfway up the door. The blood is running down in tiny rivulets and it glistens in the first light. It is dark, dark red, almost black. There are bits of something stuck in the blood spot, small gobs of...something...

Next, I register True's screams as she bursts from behind the curtain and hurls herself toward the door. I push past Pepper and stumble over the end of the couch, trying to get to her, but Trooper Stiles grabs her first. He has put an arm out, preventing her from going out the door and with his other hand he's pulling it closed. I'm up and across the small space helping to hold True back and am just in time for a last glimpse out the door as Stiles closes it.

The heads of the murdered, twin Park Rangers are lying in the sand.

***

"They're devils! They're monstrous devils!" Roger says. He's holding the wad of bloodied cloth to his forehead. It had started bleeding again when he'd jumped up from the cot at hearing True's screams.

True's elbows are on the table, her head in her hands. Stiles is still next to the door, gun out. Roger is sitting across from True and I'm sitting next to her. I don't comfort her this time, though. I know she doesn't want it. She is getting herself back together and a comforting arm might interfere with her process. I'm pretty sure that's what she's thinking. Or maybe I'm just too embarrassed to put my arm around her in front of Stiles and Roger. What if she throws it off? Huh-uh...too risky.

At Roger's words, her head comes up. "Maybe that's where it came from," she said. "The legend, I mean, The Jersey Devil legend. Maybe it's been these things, these animals, all along."

"Or maybe they *are* devils. Maybe they really are..." Roger trails off and drops his hand to consider the bloodied rag he holds. "Animals wouldn't do the things they've done. Murdering and cutting heads off just to...to torment us..."

True sits back, her eyes deep with sorrow. "Maybe it's not meant as a torment. Maybe it's meant more as a warning…maybe they're telling us to get out of their woods. Just like when people put dried deer blood around their gardens."

Gross; dried deer blood? See, this is exactly why I stay in the hospital.

She has a point, not much good it will do us.

But I'm not even sure it's true.

Trooper Stiles says what has just occurred to me: "But they *stopped* us from leaving yesterday. When they knocked the tree down in our path. *If* they knocked it down."

"I'm pretty sure they knocked it down somehow. It's a little too convenient to have been coincidence." True sighs. "I don't know why they stopped us. Maybe because we'd left Roger and Pepper behind? Maybe they wanted us to stay so they could corral us all together in one spot. I don't know."

"Not that it matters," Stiles says from his place by the door.

I'm not sure that's true, either. But I keep my mouth shut.

"I'll ride out on Pepper," Roger says into the silence, and his voice is strong, decisive. But the look on his face is cautious and scared. "We can make good time. Blow right past whatever is out there."

Stiles is shaking his head. "We get into trouble when we split up or get too far from each other. We can't split up again. How many of those things were out there? Two? Three at the most? We have the numbers if we stick together."

"You can't know that," True says. "Only Pepper was that close to them. Even Roger never really saw, did you Roger?" Roger shakes his head as True continues. "Too bad Pepper can't speak English."

"She can, kind of," I say, my voice low. I'm reluctant to do this again, but if it could help...

Trooper Stiles snorts and it's halfway between amusement and frustration. "Yeah, all horses speak a little English, don't you know that?"

It isn't clear who he's addressing. Maybe himself.

"I mean that I can translate for her," I say. "A little, anyway. I did it for a second this morning while everyone was asleep."

Even though I'm looking at my hands in my lap, I feel three sets of eyes on me. Their shock is like pinpricks on my skin. Hurts a bit. I look up and catch Stiles' eye first. He looks slightly disgusted as though I'd offered to impregnate the horse rather than just read her. But then I look at Roger and his gaze registers awe and envy–he'd never be able to commune with Pepper they way I was offering to.

Then I look to True and she's smiling and her smile says: *I knew you could do it.*

"I'm not promising anything," I caution, but True is nodding and Roger's on his feet, excited. He pulls me out of my chair and turns me to Pepper.

"Can you ask her..." he glances back at Stiles and lowers his voice, "ask her if she, you know, if she likes me?"

I know Trooper Stiles can hear Roger's request, but Roger's voice is so tinged with heartfelt concern, only the most cynical and hardened law official would have laughed...and Stiles is far from hardened. Or cynical.

"I can already tell you that, Roger. She thinks of you as family." I don't tell him that she thinks of *any* beings of sustained association as family...there's no need to deflate him. His face is pink with pleasure and also, I'd swear to it, a hint of relief. I guess he's had some guilt about Pepper assuming the burden of his weight.

He's nodding, and he takes Pepper's large head in both hands and draws it up so he can plant a kiss on her nose. Now his voice is low enough that only I can hear it. Well, Pepper and me. "I feel the same way, dear heart; you're my family, too."

"Okay, let me try this," I say and indicate to Roger that he should go back to his chair. I don't want to end up feeling like Roger is kissing *me* on *my* nose. I like Roger and all, but, no thanks, you know?

I stand in front of Pepper and take her head in my hands, similar to how Roger did it. I don't kiss her on the nose, though; I want to see into her eyes. At first I get nothing, just soft horse fur in my hands. She really is awfully soft. Her breath pulses across my bared wrists and it is warm, a little moist. Her nostrils are huge and the skin of her nose looks even softer than her fur, or is it hair? I don't know. Her eyes are deeply brown with huge irises. They are shot through with gold flecks. It is as though sunlight dapples them from somewhere beyond my power of sight, as though this horse, maybe all horses, exist under different conditions than we humans. Her eye blinks and her lashes are long and black, and I can't imagine what it's like to see from such big eyes and then she blinks again but it is slow, slow, so agonizingly slow as though time has ground down almost to a halt and then I close my own eyes and...

...I open them again and it is near dark but that doesn't bother me. I can see almost as well as I can in pure sunlight, a little better now, perhaps. I am bothered by the rustling and stirring around us, I'm not sure why the being on my back is not afraid, but he is not. So I try not to be, either. I take his lead in all things. He is my leader. But it is almost as though he does not hear what I hear: the low calling to and fro of the creatures on either side of us. My family—this current family— is strung out behind me and their tension is palpable, but it is only a ready-to-be-afraid tension, as though they do not realize the danger we are in. I try not to be afraid. The being on my back, my leader, whispers into my ear, the mystical sounds of "steady, steady" and I understand the tone, the admonition to remain calm. So I try. There is a creature directly before us and the being on my back urges me forward...the

pressure on my ribs is a command to go, go, steady, steady and I try, I do try. Then we are above the creature and it reaches for my front legs and I have no choice, I rear and stamp down, and rear again and stamp down. The weight on my back makes it impossible to jump as I need to and then another creature is under me with the first and I rear up again, as high as I can and the weight falls from my back. I jump and stamp and kick, everywhere I am grabbed, I kick out, connecting with the creatures that now surround me. I rear back and kick out with my back legs and their claws dig in, trying to stay my legs, and I kick harder, my flesh tearing. I know I am in a fight for my life, but I am not afraid. I am aware that my family is running and I will run with them. As soon as I get my legs free from the stinging biting horrors that have come from the ground. I am tired but it doesn't matter, I still fight. I know that I will fight until I break free or until my heart bursts in my chest, I will fight and fight. And suddenly I am free and I turn and run in the direction my family took, but they are gone, they've gone into the woods and now the panic comes. The panic of having lost my family and it is made worse by the pain in my legs, but still I run, the family is the most important, the most important thing, the family is survival, the family…

"…is survival," I say. My voice is rough and guttural, and I open my eyes. I release Pepper's head. Her eye is huge and panicked. Her flesh shivers and twitches on her body, her barrel chest expanding and contracting like a bellows. She was reliving the memory as I felt it with her.

"Survival, Pepper," I tell her. "The family is survival." I realize I'm not 100% back and then I'm awash in vertigo and tipping over…into Roger's arms and he guides me to the floor.

"JD? Are you okay, son?" Roger asks.

"My arms sting," I say, barely mumbling and then I am gone for a bit.

***

When I come to, the first thing I see is True's smile in her beautiful face. My family; she is my family.

"You're so beautiful," I tell her. "I love you."

There is a snort somewhere behind me but I don't care. I continue to smile at True.

"He's okay," a voice says, and it's the voice of the snorter. Rude bastard.

"Stiles, you rude bastard," I say and he laughs.

"Come on, JD, snap out of it. Tell us what you saw." He's behind True, looking down at me. I realize I'm lying on the floor. I put my hand out to Stiles.

"Help me up," I say and he does.

"Steady now," he says as I list and tilt my way to the table. This is odd. I've never been so disoriented from a vision. Then again, I've never gone into the mind of a horse.

Just as I am about to sit, True says, "JD, be careful of your arms."

I look at my sleeves. They're dotted with blood. It's not too bad; just stings a little. I settle into the chair, gingerly keeping my arms away from the rough wood surface of the tabletop. I look around at my 'family' and I smile. I'm sure it's a terse, sad smile. True takes a hesitant step closer then stops.

"They come up from the ground," I tell them. "We're in trouble."

Christine Dougherty

-17-

"I still think it's best if I ride out on Pepper. She's fast and I'm sure she can outrun anything that lives underground. You three can stay here until I bring back help. Stiles, you can defend this cabin, can't you?" Roger seems surer of himself. Maybe it's because now he knows the depths of Pepper's commitment to him. Or maybe his head just doesn't hurt as much and he's back to his true self.

"I don't think they 'live' underground, exactly," I say. "They just *attack* from the ground in some way. They're enmeshed in the brush...not under the dirt." Remembering the grimy faces of the creatures as seen through Pepper's memory gives me the shivers. Their foreheads were large with odd, bony protrusions above the eyes–I'd got that part right– but their faces and bodies weren't covered with fur as I'd first thought...they were covered with grass, pine needles, sand, and dirt. There was hair of a sort on their heads, but it, too, was tangled with pine needles and sticks. Their eyes were the worst. There was no discernable pupil or iris, just black, blind-looking orbs rimmed with a red so bloody looking, they appeared to be injured. Each of their eight fingers ended in a strong, yet somewhat translucent, claw. I glanced up at the window–the dirty, yellow plastic is almost the exact shade of their nails, almost the exact opacity.

I shake my head. "I don't think Pepper's any safer than we are. She's vulnerable *because* of her legs, actually. I'm sure that's why they were grabbing for her."

"I don't understand what you mean, JD," Roger says.

"Their claws are not strong enough to go easily through heavier material like our jeans and pants and for sure not our boots. Pepper's legs are bare. Andrew's and Jackson's legs were bare, too."

True's brows draw together and I know she's recalling how the twins were dressed yesterday. Their shorts were green, almost knee length, and their boots came to just above their ankles exposing a good portion of their calves, shins, and knees. True and Roger are each in long pants made of heavy cotton. Stiles is in his blue uniform pants, also long and heavy, and I'm wearing jeans.

Roger shakes his head. "You can't be killed by having your legs scratched up. That wouldn't kill a man or a horse."

"No, not just a few scratches, that's true, but if they can get at you enough, keep scratching and tearing at you until you panicked, it would make you vulnerable, maybe you'd fall and then..." I don't want to say the rest. Picturing it is bad enough.

"Then they'd get at your face and neck. Maybe even your jugular. That's why the twins were so bloody." True's voice is calm. It seems she has regained her composure. I am again filled with admiration for her, and something more, something warmer than admiration. Whoa. I'm really digging this girl. It's a complication I could do without right now.

"Listen…" Trooper Stiles says. He's back at his post by the door, but looking down at the rough, wooden planks that make up the floor of the cabin. We all fall into silence, and I hear it…a sshhh sound like a heavy cloth bag being dragged slowly across the underside of the floor.

Pepper blows and stamps her front feet nervously and the sound stops. Roger reaches to put a calming hand on Pepper's neck.

I hear it again: shhhhhhhh…it is a stealthy, sneaky sound.

Stiles motions to an area on the far side of the little table, where he thinks the noise is coming from. I raise my shoulders at him, *what now?* And he shakes his head helplessly. The noise comes again, but this time it's on the far side of the cabin, in the living room area. At least two of them, then. Maybe more.

Then the noise comes again, directly under my feet. I look down. There are some good-sized cracks between the planks and a knothole large enough to stick a thumb through. Something moves past but it's dark down there, pitch black. I wave my arm to get Stiles' attention and then point straight down at my feet. I pantomime a shooting gesture at the floor.

Stiles shakes his head and mouths *no, too dangerous,* meaning it's too dangerous to shoot through the floor in these tight quarters. Who knows where the bullet might ricochet?

I shake my head and then put my thumb and finger to-gether in an 'okay' symbol and hold it up to Stiles…*there's a hole in the floor this big*…I mouth and then point down again.

Stiles nods his understanding. He's only four feet from where I sit, but he'll have to come around the table to get to me.

For a big guy, Stiles is awfully quiet as he closes the space between us. He tiptoes across, the heels of his Trooper shoes never touching the floor. Now he can see the knot at my feet and we both look down into it. Yes, something is moving down there. It brushes up against the hole and pauses. It is grayish brown, but I can't make any other kind of judgment about it beyond that, but something tells me this is one of our dirt monsters. Stiles cups a hand over his ear and looks around at the three of us. We all put our hands over our ears and I cautiously draw my feet up and away, practically squat-ting on the chair.

Stiles leans over, his neck and shoulders straining. He looks like a muscular vulture. He holds the gun about two feet from the hole and sights down the barrel. He can't put it right up against the hole; the thing under there would see or hear it for sure.

My attention is focused on Stiles' trigger finger, and as he depresses it, I cringe back in the chair. Just as an aside–as much as I dislike the great outdoors, I dislike loud noises even more. Nora says she thinks this, too, is related to being blasted from my home as a baby. Maybe, maybe not…but one thing I am sure of: that gun is going to be loud.

And, man, am I ever right about that.

Before my ears even get a chance to fully register the blast, the hole in the floor suddenly develops jagged, splinter-throwing edges. The knot is now at least four times as big. I could put my hand through it. Not that I'd be that crazy.

As soon as the blast dies away, an ungodly screaming/whistling noise takes its place. The sound is like the Devil's own teakettle and let me tell you, he's brewing up a pot of trouble. I had been taking my hands away from my ears, but now I cover them again. The wail from under the floorboards is so piercing I'm surprised our ears aren't bleeding. Then it dies away.

There's a scuttling, bumping commotion under the floor on the far side of the cabin…seems our other guest has beat a hasty retreat. True takes three quick strides to the milky-eyed window and pulls the plastic back by an inch–just enough to peek out.

"It just ran into the woods!" Her tone is excited triumph. Then: "Hey…" she says, her voice fading in its surprise. She turns back to us and shakes her head. She looks dazed. "It didn't look…it looked…" She shakes her head again.

"True?" Roger says. "What's wrong? What did you see?"

She shakes her head a third time. "I don't know." She looks to me, dazed. "JD, in your vision, did they look…were they…this sounds weird, but…were they kind of…made of dirt?"

"Dirty?" Roger asks in head-tilted confusion.

"No, not dirty…*made* of dirt, did they look like they were…" she trails off and raises her shoulders helplessly, at a loss to explain further.

Her words stir something in my memory. Something about their eyes and claws, they were wrong or…not *wrong*, exactly, just not *natural*. I open my mouth to ask her for clarification, hoping to jog my memory even more, but Stiles speaks before I get a chance.

"Huh. That's weird."

We turn to look at him. He has his hand in the hole made by the bullet. The sight of his arm wrist deep in that hole gives me a start; it's almost like seeing someone with his hand in a garbage disposal–probably nothing is going to happen, but geez, you just never know.

"Get your hand out of there…what if that thing is still alive?" Roger says. He must have had the same uneasy association I'd had.

The Trooper doesn't even look up. He twists his arm and pulls it back out of the hole. He opens his clenched fist and a stream of dirt, pine needles, and sand funnels onto the floor. He looks up, his features contorted in confusion.

"I guess I missed," he says, but his tone voices another opinion, the opinion that he *couldn't* have missed…not at such close range. "What the hell *are* these things?" he asks, and now he sounds almost angry. I don't blame him. I know how it feels to have your beliefs ripped out from under you. The world becomes a shifting, uneven puzzle from there on out.

I shake my head and glance at True. She shrugs. She and I are the only ones who've gotten a good look at these things. Neither of us wants to say what we're really thinking.

"Okay, look, this is the time to make a move, while those things are on the run," Roger says. He's already twining a hand through the reins on Pepper's bridle, getting ready to lead her out. Stiles nods and stands, brushing the remaining dirt form his hands.

"Yeah, you're right. We should head out right now."

True nods her agreement.

I swallow. Hard. Feels like my heart is trying to climb out through my esophagus. I don't want to go out there and get scratched to death by dirt monsters. But I'm not gonna hang out in this cabin by myself, either.

Seems as though I haven't much choice.

So I nod, too, and then I open the door.

***

As I exit the cabin, the dawn light is starting to work its way through the dense canopy of pine needles. The birds, just beginning to stir, are peeping sleepily. The air is freakishly cool for July. Behind me, True gasps in surprise.

I turn to her, my stomach dropping, but she's looking past me and down. I follow her gaze. The entire forest floor is swirled with an eerie ground fog. It is ghostly in the half-light and almost seems to squirm over the bed of sand and pine needles and weaves heavily through the stands of mountain laurel. I hadn't noticed because I was so busy looking for the sun.

Anything could hide under that cover of fog…anything.

I turn to try and force my way back into the cabin, but I'm too late. True has brushed past me but now Roger and Pepper have blocked the doorway. Very effectively. Horses, even small ones, tend to be good door blockers. I only get one arm squeezed past her and back into the cabin. Great.

Roger glances at me in confusion and a bit of consterna-tion.

"What are you doing?" he asks.

I glance at True and then back to Roger. Okay, I'm start-ing to look like a psycho again. Gotta get my act together over here. I shake my head. "Nothing. It's nothing." I with-draw my arm and join True. She smiles and takes my hand and squeezes it.

"Don't worry," she says. "We just have to stick together. Nothing will happen as long as we all stick–"

A boom cuts her off and she ducks instinctively, pulling

me down with her. Pepper, who'd been about halfway through the door, jumps violently and pushes forward. Roger is bunted aside but he manages to keep his feet...and her reins.

True turns back to the cabin, orienting on the sound faster than I do. It was a gunshot. Only one person out here has a gun. What I hear next will haunt me as long as I live–although at this point, I'm guessing I only have maybe another two minutes.

Trooper Stiles is screaming. A bull-throated roar of fear and pain.

True's face is a frozen mask of white dread and Roger is still struggling with Pepper's reins. It's on me, then. I stand and leap through the cabin door.

Stiles is waist deep in a hole in the floor. What had been a quarter-sized knothole, then a fist sized blow-hole, is now the size of a manhole cover and growing. The edges are being bit and torn at even as I see Stiles' uniform blouse shredding where it meets the hole. His face is written in stark lines of terror, veins are popping out on his neck, and his throat is a red bulge as he yells. I stand frozen as his eyes find mine. His screaming doesn't stop even as another blast comes from beneath the floorboards. I notice that his right arm is also below the floor, and he must still be holding the gun because the floor is lit with a yellow flash. He's shooting at whatever has him.

"JD, help me," he says, rasping it out and then he's screaming again. Three more booms and flashes and suddenly he slips in chest deep. It's almost like watching someone pulled into quicksand. But much worse...*so* much worse. The edges of his shirt are now red with blood and it flicks and spatters upward, dotting his neck and the underside of his chin. I swallow and shake my head. Then I step forward and take his hand...

...my legs are immediately consumed by fire and it reaches my stomach and then my chest, burning and tearing, the pain is unimaginable, without precedent in my life or in Stiles' and then I get a flash of an older lady, Stiles' mother, my mother, and she is home waiting for me she's been sick a long time and I take care of her and she is afraid every time I leave for work and I always tell her that I'll be fine and she worries too much and then I give her a kiss on the cheek and she smiles, mom, oh mom, I'm so sorry, who will take care of you now, mom? Who will do it now that I...

I wrench myself back, dropping Stiles' hand. I can't pull him out when I'm touching him and I can't pull him out *without* touching him...I turn and scan the cabin, the image of quicksand still in my mind. I tip a chair over at Stiles' chest and he reaches for it. He is almost shoulders deep now, only his left arm flailing free. He's not yelling anymore, he is thinking of his mother, vowing to get himself out and safe for her sake. He wraps his arm around the chair and his face becomes red and straining with effort; spit bursts from his lips in a small spray as he pulls.

He's not gonna make it.

True brushes past me and throws herself to her knees at Stiles' side. Her arms wrap around his neck and under one armpit and she leans back, screaming in her panicked attempt to single handedly pull Stiles free of the hole. She actually manages to lift him by a few inches and what is exposed is Stiles' chest and it looks…chewed, shredded. I feel my gorge rise. Then Roger is past me and he stuffs a braided lanyard into Stiles' hand.

"Hold this, hold it tight!" Roger says, yelling into Stiles' dazed and uncomprehending face. "Hold it Stiles, like this!" He curls Stiles' fist around the rope. "Slap her!" Roger says to me as he joins True in her Herculean effort. "Slap her ass!"

I turn and stumble out the door, being careful not to get the lead between the horse and me. I slap Pepper's ass with a force fueled by fear and she leaps straight up and then tries to take off running. The rope pulls taut and for one agonizing moment Pepper is held in place. Then she is moving, pulling forward, snorting, her hooves digging deep divots in the sand. It's working. She's dragging Stiles out of the hole. A burst of triumph courses through me and then all at once, the rope goes slack, giving Pepper her head. Amazingly, she doesn't take off.

I bend to grab her dragging reins and coax her back into

the cabin. I push through the door and then pause, shaken by the sight. It's a sorry one.

Stiles has been pulled free of the hole, but he's covered in blood from the chest down. His clothes are ripped and torn; below his knees, they are effectively gone, just a few blue shreds hanging here and there. He still holds the gun in his right hand. Roger pulls it from his weakening grip. He leans to Stiles' ear. "You're okay, just take it easy. You'll be all right." A lie. There's no way Stiles is going to be all right. He's half dead, and we're still here…stuck in these woods.

True is leaning over the hole, her face set in lines of caution.

"True, get away from there," I say, but she only glances at me and then returns her attention to the hole. Before I can do anything, she squats and goes feet-first through the floor-boards. Is she crazy? The floorboards are still streaked with gore and she's what? Going after the creatures? I know she's brave, but that's ridiculous!

Before I can get to where she is, she pops back up, her hands on the edges, and lifts herself out. "True, dammit, what are you doing? Aren't things bad enough?" Roger says. He has taken the wadded rag from his head and is trying to staunch the blood of Stiles' uncountable wounds. Stiles groans and tries to roll over. "Stiles, be still, don't struggle." Roger looks at True again, an emotion almost as strong as fury in his eyes. "Get out of there, True."

"I found this," True says and uncurls her fist. A bit of

white flashes, tumbling from her hand and landing with a soft clunk. She immediately brushes her hands against her pants as if trying to rid them of something nastier than mere dirt.

Roger and I bend over what she found in the hole.

It's a molar and it is wound in a thin braid of dark hair. The hair is knotted in a rough bow. It looks almost tribal, or like something from Voodoo. It is *immensely* creepy.

"That's human. A human tooth," Roger says. I don't want to know how he knows. I back away from it.

"We have to get out," I say. "There's something really wrong here." I can't explain to them the feeling that is coming over me, but I'm suddenly awash in a sense of unreality, as though this isn't happening. I feel like I'm locked in a dream with nightmarish overtones.

Roger's eyes are on me, burning into my skin. I know what he's about to ask. This is even worse than Stiles wanting me to touch the murdered twins. I feel like I'd rather die than–

"JD, you have to," Roger says, reaching out. It's obvious that I already know what he's asking. I step back, shaking my head. No way. Huh-uh. Forget it. His hand is on my arm. "You have to, JD; you know you have to. I wouldn't ask if it wasn't…" He glances at Stiles. "If it wasn't really, really important." He doesn't say life or death important, but I know he's thinking it. Life or death important. What about my life? I want to ask him. But I don't. He's right, of course.

I look at True. Her expression is neutral but unwavering. She has a better idea of the cost to me, and her eyes tell me she is behind me no matter what I decide.

I decide.

I bend forward again and pinch the tooth with the very tips of my fingers. An odd jolt runs up my arm and I'm forced to drop it. That pisses me off a little and I frown down. Then I grasp it fully, as though it were a mouse I was catching, and for the briefest instant it seems to squirm–to change–in my hand. In my surprise, I almost drop it again but instead clench my fist tight. The soft edges bite into my palm and the hair shifts, tickling. I can't tell if the movement is in my head– part of an impending vision–or if it's really happening.

I glance at True to see…

…a deep rushing blackness a whistling hole where I should be there is nothing, a living nothingness, a walking contradiction a sense of nothing save a twisted hatred, a hunger of the soul, a desire for acquisition and a burning greed, a deep sense of greed and jealousy, jealous rage and blackness, emptiness and a whistling hole where I should be, a sudden stinging sensation on my wrist and I am…

…back in the cabin with True, her arms around me. She is shaking or I am shaking or maybe we both shake. I can't tell and I don't care. I wrap my arms around her. I've never felt so happy–so relieved–to be out of a vision.

"That was…that was bad," I say, my teeth chattering.

"I've never felt anything like that."

"What was it? What did you feel?" she asks, making no move to pull away. If anything, she holds me tighter.

"Nothing…nothingness," I say, knowing it makes no sense. "It was the opposite of being alive, except not dead. I didn't feel like anything, I mean, I didn't feel like I *was* anything."

"You were mumbling that you would kill us, you kept saying it: 'going to kill you, going to kill you, you have what I want and I will kill you.' Your eyes were…they looked dead, empty. It scared me."

Her words give me a jolt, they are so close to what I was thinking, no–not thinking, visioning.

"It wasn't human," I say and finally am able to pull back from her. "Whatever it was, it wasn't human. It wasn't alive."

"JD, that makes no sense," Roger says. He's still on the floor next to Stiles. He's looking at me in perplexed bewilderment.

"They're monsters." Trooper Stiles' voice–slurred and somehow blurry–startles us all. He sighs and tries to roll over. Roger helps him, hissing in sympathy when Stiles groans. "They're made of dirt."

Roger tilts his head as though he thinks he heard Stiles wrong. "Dirty?" he asks, the same as he'd asked of True earlier.

Stiles shakes his head, a slow and laborious process. His

eyes are closed. "No, not dirty. Made of dirt. Sticks and dirt. And sand. But strong. They're really...really strong."

"How can something be 'made of dirt'? It doesn't make any sense." He looks up at True and me and his eyes are pleading. "Does that make any sense to you?"

Before I can answer, True is nodding her head. "Yes. Now that he said it, it makes sense. It's what I saw out the window."

I nod, too. "That must be why it felt so empty. So devoid of a soul or anything even remotely human or in possession of humanity."

Roger lowers his head and his shoulders droop in defeat. He sits back and crosses his legs Indian style. Then he fishes a black stone from his pocket and stares at it.

"I know what it is," he says, looking up. His eyes are ringed with dark and his face has drained of color. "And it's not good."

Well, I could have told him that much.

***

Roger and I are pushing Stiles up onto Pepper's back. True is on the other side, pulling him into place. He finally sits in the saddle, but barely. He slumps over, his hands slack on the pommel.

"It's similar to the Dybbuk from Hebrew folklore, and

there is something similar in Catholicism called a Golgothan, but the Shawnee Indians called it a Dalakihillen, or a Killen for short. It's made for the purpose of revenge or protection against enemies. The one who conjures the demon, usually the Medicine man, is said to put a spark of his own soul into a carefully selected and consecrated pile of dirt and sticks; sometimes in the lore it's mud, sometimes human waste." He glances apologetically at True, but she isn't even looking at him. She's leading Pepper as Roger and I bolster Stiles on either side.

I'm pretty grossed out, though. Human waste? That's just out of the question, as far as I'm concerned.

"When the Medicine man is split like that, he's in a vulnerable position...especially if he's split himself into two or more Killen; I'm only surmising that last bit because I've actually never heard of anyone putting themselves into more than one. You know, this area was once populated with Native Americans. The Lenni-Lenape or 'Original People' were settled onto one of the first 'Indian reservations' in the 1700s. It was called Brotherton. There's been a lot of bad blood since then, but I don't think there are any Native Americans in this area anymore." The regret in his voice is tangible. The crow's feather tucked into his hatband is ragged and dusty since his tumble from Pepper.

The sun is almost fully up and the ground fog is burning off. The odd chill has been burned off, too, with the sun reestablishing itself as the King of Summer. While yesterday I decried the heat, this morning I welcome it gratefully.

Heat gives you a sense of life. Even if it's illusory.

I scan the ground on my side of Pepper. It's a little easier now that we know where to look. But will they always come from the ground? That, my friends, is a good question.

"Roger, are you part Native American?" I remember True saying something about it earlier, but I can't remember what, exactly, she said. I think some conversation will keep my mind from wandering itself to the blackest, worst case scenario the way it seems to want to.

I see the feather bob. "One sixteenth on my Mother's side."

I thought he'd have more to say about it, but he remains quiet. I cast around, trying to think of something else to ask him, but he beats me to the punch.

"Why do you live in that hospital, JD? You seem okay," he says and glances over Pepper's neck. It's a strange question, almost like he's trying to deflect, and it catches me off-guard. In my peripheral vision, I see True glance back, then turn quickly forward again. I can tell she's listening.

My face colors.

"It's easier. It's orderly. Everything happens on a schedule and that…it suits me, it suits my nature. I'm not very adventurous."

"How long have you lived there?" Roger asks.

"For nine years, since I was sixteen. Since my aunt died."

"You lived with your aunt before she passed?"

I nod. It's all I can do. I'm not going to get into it, especially not out here in these freaky damn woods. The things that happened before now, before Aunt Mayella's death, are better off not talked about. She had gotten very paranoid, especially in the year before the accident took her away. I know that she had started 'investigating' my parents' death...her words...but she hadn't shared anything specific with me.

Some of her paranoia stemmed from what I'd started being able to do right around age fourteen–when the psychic ability started to kick in. By fifteen, I was rocking and rolling with it and (this shames me, now), I used it more for bad than for good. It was easy to manipulate people when you knew their secrets, and I manipulated like a puppet master. What the hell, okay? I was only fifteen. And not the happiest of kids, either.

I don't know why Aunt Mayella started to think my abilities had something to do with my parents' death. She never got around to telling me, even though she had promised she would when she 'had something concrete' to say.

Nora and I had discussed some of it–my shame and my suspicions–in detail when I first came to live in the hospital. But since that first year, I've tried my best to stop thinking about it, about any of it.

Nothing changes the past.

"What about your parents, JD? Where are they?"

"Dead," I say, and True glances back at me again, concerned.

Roger waits to see if I'll say more, but I don't. I'm done with that topic.

"True? What do you think? Are we getting near the path?"

She hesitates as if deciding whether to pursue the subject of my parents' death or not, then she answers.

"I don't know for sure. I can't judge it on time because yesterday was so disjointed. Especially after those things–those creatures–attacked us." She stumbles just a bit over 'those creatures' and I know she is avoiding calling them Killen...either because she doesn't believe or because she doesn't want to give a name to what is frightening her. "If we just keep going east, we'll come to it, that's a given. I just don't know when. I also don't know how far down we'll be once we get to the trail. It's not necessarily going to be smooth sailing once we get there, either."

"I think they'll leave us alone once they realize we're leaving. It has to be territorial in some fashion. Whoever sent these things must believe we're a danger to them. We're the interlopers, after all."

I don't like Roger's reasoning; it has an almost concerned bent towards the creatures–Killen as he thinks. In my mind, there is nothing noble about a mud man. Plus, how could

Roger dismiss what had happened to Trooper Stiles, much less to the twins? His sympathies seemed misplaced. Weirdly so.

We all fall silent. The loudest sound is Pepper's hooves breaking small twigs and even that wasn't very loud at all. The woods seem a little less creepy now that the morning sun is fully up. It's a cheerful yellow and it lights on the flitting moths that—

Pepper screams and rears up, throwing Stiles from his precarious spot on her back and into a stand of wild blueberries. The reins rip through True's hand and she turns, hissing in pain but still tries to grab the whipping twin cords. Roger is bunted to the ground as Pepper faints left, her hooves stomping blurs of motion. I grab at the rein nearest me and it snaps back across my face, burning like a whip crack. Now I am bunted aside as Pepper sidesteps toward me. She's still screaming. Her eyes are round with terror. I try to see down past her feet and then I scan the brush on either side. Nothing. Nothing is there.

True has finally grabbed both reins and Roger staggers upright, coming toward the panicked horse. "Whoa, whoa, Pepper, easy now girl, take it easy girl…"

His voice is calm and even, and Pepper turns her rolling eye toward him. She whinnies shrilly and stamps a front hoof. Her back and sides are covered with sweat. Those deep patches detail the depths of her terror, but she is calming down. I'm afraid to put my hand on her. It might make things worse.

True waits until Roger is caressing Pepper's neck and then she comes closer, looping the reins over her arm. She puts a hand on Pepper's nose and the horse swings her head up but then brings it immediately back down, acquiescing to True's touch.

My heart is beating so hard I can hear it in my ears. Did Pepper see one of the creatures or did something else spook her? I take a breath, trying to gather up my galloping thoughts. Then I remember Stiles and I look back.

He isn't there.

***

"Where could he have gone? He couldn't have gone any-where!" True questions and answers herself, her voice climbing through the registers. Her eyes are wide and roll in a way eerily similar to Pepper's. "He was hurt, really hurt! JD? Roger? You saw how hurt he was! He couldn't have just–"

"True." Roger cuts her off. His voice is calm, as calm as it was when he was gentling Pepper, and True's mouth closes with a snap. "The Killen got him. I'm sure of it. They planned it. They scared Pepper to make Stiles fall and that kept us busy while they dragged Stiles away. Look." He indicates a large set of drag marks that leads into and out of the nearby underbrush. "We have to act quickly; they can't be very far yet. Let's go."

Go? Is he kidding? We're almost at that trail! We're almost out!

But of course, he's right. Stiles would do the same for me, for any of us.

Roger starts out and True falls in behind him leading Pepper. I for sure don't want to be last so I trot up next to True.

"You're going to let him track?" I keep my voice very low. I wouldn't want to hurt Roger's feelings. "You said you were a better tracker."

She glances at me with the ghost of a smile. "I'm watching," she says. "But you really can't miss the trail they left. Stiles was a big guy and they haven't had the time to cover their tracks."

"Is."

"Is?"

"Stiles *is* a big guy," I say and shrug, embarrassed. "It just gave me a jolt when you said...I just meant that..."

True reaches out and squeezes my hand.

"Is. Of course. He *is* a big guy. Listen, JD, everything is going to be fine, okay? We'll find him."

I like True a lot, I think that's obvious, but I'm tired of everyone reassuring me that everything will be fine...nothing has been fine since I stepped into these woods. I *never* should have left the hospital.

Mentally, I give myself a shake. Self-pity won't get me anywhere. I've done pretty well so far, right? Better than I ever would have thought, that's for sure. Wait till I tell Nora. She won't believe even half of it. My room at the hospital comes into my mind and I picture Nora sitting, open mouthed with awe as I tell her everything that happened. I know she'll even have a bit of guilt over forcing me to do this, especially after I show her my various injuries. For a minute, her imagined guilt gives me a glow of satisfaction…she'll think twice about handing me clippings from here on out, in fact–

I nearly walk right into Roger.

His back is still to us, but he's looking left in the direction of the morning sun. He flaps his hand in a 'get down' gesture even as he lowers himself to a squat.

Uh, hello? I feel like saying, what about the horse? We could lay flat on the ground and someone would still see Pepper standing there…she doesn't exactly blend.

Then I turn in astonishment at a creak of leather from behind me. Pepper has gone to her knees and laboriously, carefully and with effort, she folds her legs under and lies down among the blueberry bushes.

"JD, you get down, too," Roger says and I turn back to him. There is a glint of amused pride in his eyes. He raises his eyebrows. "She's some horse, huh?"

I squat and nod, and Roger smiles, but he sobers quickly and turns away.

"I see a cabin. Do you see it? About fifty yards straight

ahead."

I squint in the direction he's pointing. He's got good eyes; I'd never have noticed that cabin. It seems to merge right into the forest around it.

"The trail is heading right for it," he says.

"Roger, I'm glad you were leading. I'd never have seen that cabin," True says, and there is honest admiration in her voice.

Roger turns again and smiles in brief acknowledgement. But there is a flash of something more...something almost like shame. But that makes no sense.

"Well," I say. "Now what?"

Roger glances at me and this time there's a different glint in his eye: speculative, reckless, and brave...a kind of 'damn the torpedoes, full steam ahead' look.

"Now we go get Stiles."

I consider him for a moment, feeling my fear at war with something new, a new feeling...not bravery exactly, but willingness...a willingness to go along with the team, to throw myself into battle without reservation. Well, *some* reservation, this is still me, after all; I didn't morph into Rambo overnight. But it still feels good. I nod.

"Okay, let's go."

Christine Dougherty

-18-

We had to leave Pepper behind; we didn't have a choice, but the fact of Pepper's potential vulnerability weighs heavily on Roger. I don't think Pepper is as vulnerable as he thinks. When I'd gone into Pepper's mind, when I'd experienced a little bit of what it's like to be a horse, the thing that I'd come out with was the confident feeling of bulky–yet somehow fleet and graceful–strength. I couldn't explain it if I tried. Not to Roger. Pepper is his baby; the child he never had. He worries about her because that is what a good parent does…they fret and fuss and pray for the best.

Not that I would know.

We are less than twenty feet from the cabin. Seen up close, it can barely even be called that. It's more of a shack. The outer walls are constructed of planks weathered a mottled gray like field stone and are covered here and there with thick patches of grayish green moss. More moss, a lighter green and growing in small mounds, covers the entire roof. It would be impossible to say what the roof's original construction material had been.

There are two small windows on the side of the cabin we face, but they are dark, blank eyes, giving no hint to what lies within.

True taps on Roger's shoulder and when he turns to her

she mouths: *Leeds' cabin?* Her features drawn down in concern. Roger shrugs and shakes his head, his meaning obvious: *Maybe. I don't know.*

I'd done my share of reading on the Jersey Devil and the accounts were so varied, so contradictory, it was hard to understand where the original legend had come from. Some stories held Mrs. Leeds as a witch, others told of a Demon baby that she gave back to Satan, still others said that the Leeds baby was a deformed child held in a basement until such time as it broke free to terrify the surrounding homesteads.

But in any case, the stories go back as far at the 17th century—this cabin was dilapidated, but not three hundred plus years old. I think True and Roger are starting to feed into each other's hysteria.

"Listen, guys," I say, my voice lower than a whisper. "Let's not get too crazy, here, okay? There's no way this can be the old Leeds' cabin. That cabin—if it ever even existed—would be dust by now, it would have been termite food long since."

True's brows drew closer together the more I talked. For a moment, I thought she was getting angry but then a sort of realization dawned on her features and she shot Roger a look, a smile tucked into the corner of her mouth.

"What?" Now it's me being defensive. What was she laughing about?

"I said 'least hazard' not 'Leeds Cabin'…it's Ranger

shorthand for least hazardous way in or out of a bad situation. "I meant, what is our best route to that cabin?"

"Oh," I whisper. I nod. I feel kind of stupid, but True smiles.

"Hey, you couldn't know. How could you know?" She reaches for my hand again and squeezes my fingers. I know that this is just a habit of hers, but I like it. A lot. A *whole* lot. I smile back.

"Come on, lovebirds," Roger whispers, and I feel my face suffuse with hot, embarrassed blood. Lovebirds? Oh man, True is going to laugh her ass off at that one. I chance a glance at her. To my surprise, she's blushing, too. That's weird.

But I don't have time to contemplate further because Roger is up and crossing through the small bit of clearing around the cabin. True gives me the briefest, shyest of smiles then she is up, too, and not far behind Roger.

I stay put for three more beats of my heart.

Then I follow her.

It's a short, nerve-wracking trek. The windows look more than ever like malevolent eyes and I would swear that they track my progress. They are somehow blind yet all seeing, like a statue, an effigy, or a stone god.

Roger and True are squatting with their backs to the cabin and they both watch me carefully. I'm across to them in seconds and I bend over to catch my breath. My lungs feel weighted, shriveled...I can't get enough air. I reach out to steady myself and my hand lands on the side of the cabin and I heave in a breath and…

…I let it out, blowing with all the force of my lungs; I blow into my hand curled to my face. My hand is dark and deeply lined. It is old. I uncurl my fist and stare at the sand and sticks. The part that is still JD is surprised to see the sand begin to stir, to swirl in and around itself. Delicate lines appear, and they fan out and grow, like a root system, or like veins. The feeling in my palm is both light and tickling but also foul in the truest sense of the word. The part that is still me is sickened by the feel of it.

There are pine needles and they begin to push out, to the outer edges and they bend and twist themselves around the small sticks. The pine needles resemble tendons where they connect the sticks at the join. I roll my hand and bring it to my mouth again. I breathe out and this time, I feel something give inside. I can't tell if the tug is in my mind, my heart, or maybe my entire body. There is a sense of giving something up, something important. There is a feeling of emptiness but also release.

I breathe a part of myself into the small, moving bundle in my hand.

I lay it carefully on the ground at my feet. My feet, too, are dark and old. The bottoms are tough and the toes resemble something made of red, seamed granite. These are powerful feet that have walked the skin of the Earth for many seasons.

Powerful feet that support a powerful body, and more importantly, a powerful mind.

I look up to a ring of faces that watch with awe as the mound of dirt before me begins to grow. It is taking more dirt to itself, more sand, more sticks. It weaves itself into being. The people before me (the family, my host mind whispers) sigh as one and their eyes are round with exultation but also with fear.

They know that what their Shaman is doing is dangerous business. The Killen cannot always be controlled. There are stories told of other Tribes of People where a Killen has run wild, killing warriors, woman, elders, even children...the Killen has no mercy. Because the Killen has no heart. Nothing exists in its chest save the hard grittiness of sand.

The family falls back as the Killen continues to form but with one hard glance, the Shaman stays them. Deep inside, they'd like to go and hide in their huts, but the Shaman needs them here as much as he is himself needed. The Shaman is not a Shaman unto himself. He is bound by the strength or weakness of his People, his family.

The Killen continues to grow. Now it is the size of a toddler; now the size of a child just before puberty. Still it draws from the piles of long grasses, sand, dirt, globs of clay, sticks of every kind and size, leaves...everything the People have gathered together to feed it into being. Now it is the size of a woman; now it is the size of a man and still it grows. Sticks

171

and stones are weaved together forming tendons of such strength that the Killen will have the strength of ten warriors. It will be able to run from sun to sun, never tiring, the only sustenance it requires is the very essence of the forest it haunts. There is no end to the fodder that keeps it whole unto itself.

The Shaman rises on his old, strong legs, his robe falling open, and I feel a curious tug and then I am outside the Shaman, watching with the consciousness of the tribe. The people rise with the Shaman. Firelight licks across dark eyes and places hot kisses on copper skin.

"Aaaaaaaaaahhhhhhh," the Shaman says and it is both a note and a breath and the People sing and sigh with him. Their twined voices are plaintive and eerie in the cool night. The note echoes and reverberates under the canopy of the pines.

Now the Killen has reached its length, longer than any warrior who exists now or who ever existed. Its head is large with protrusions over its eyes. Its shoulders taper more than would be the case if it were a man of this height. The shoulders look almost pliable and they are, the Killen is able to fold itself almost flat as it pulls itself through the underbrush. Its large head breaks trail so the rest of it can slide through with ease. They are tremendously fast both above the ground and traveling low across it.

"Aaaaaaaahhhhhhhh," the Shaman and the People in-

tone again and I feel a gathering energy in the air. Night birds that had been flitting through the air and animals scurrying among the branches fall silent.

The Killen is utterly still, lying before the Shaman. The energy in the air becomes almost palpable; the body of the Shaman is wracked with small but intense tremors. The People wait, breath held, watching as one.

This is the Killen's time.

With a sound like desolate wind sighing through branches, the chest of the Killen rises, the dirt mouth opening wide to expose the black opening to its dirt throat. Its breath is harsh and dry, no juice of true life in it. It heaves in another breath and opens eyes of onyx that glitter with false life in the fire's glow.

The Killen draws a third breath and rises to sit upright and the People kneel, faces alight with fear and gratitude. This Killen will save them. It will go out into the land east of the People's home and kill what it finds there. It will keep the soldiers and government lawyers at bay. It will keep their land theirs. *No matter the odds.*

The Shaman raises his arms, palms up in supplication. The coyote head headdress he wears seems to watch the Killen with eyes just as dead. It stares without judgment.

The Killen rises.

The People cover their eyes with their hands; to look into the Killen's face is to have your soul marked for all time. I feel another tug and strange weight as though I am being pulled through black water and then I am in...

...the Killen and deep inside is a dark and whistling hole and i am cold beyond reason, i am more than dead, i was never alive. my father before me who called me into existence bids me to look upon him and i do. in my father's eyes i see some small thing that is me, twisting and strained; tethered to his will. my father bids me go to the land of east and kill what i might find there. i turn to do my father's bidding and i see a ring of people with hands covering eyes, fresh tracks of tears, and trembling as that of prey and a sudden hunger joins the hole inside me. these are the people of my father and i want...i want...what they have.

but i am bid go past and leave my father's people and i do but my eye slides over each face and finally lights upon eyes that glint back at me. the eyes are filled with awe, with fear and some miniscule bit of the hole that is my sense of myself receives a drip, a modicum of satisfaction. i want to fill myself with that awe, i want to cut the skin from this being of my father's and scratch down to where the life is...i want that life, i want to fill the whistling hole.

i am bid to not harm these people, the people of my father and i do not, but i take that modicum of awe and keep it and the small child who dared look upon me falls forward in a dead faint.

i run and the running is endless through light and dark

and light again. deer and rabbits run before me, trembling and afraid and i want to catch them and scratch down to their life force but i am bid to do my father's will and I pass by the prey animals. finally i come upon my father's enemies. all people save my father's are his enemies. as they are mine.

i kill the enemies of my father. i suck up the small bits of life that i can but they never fill the hole. i am never alive. the sorrow feeds the black rage and i find more of my father's enemies and i kill them.

and i continue on.

and then i come to a place where the pine trees end and i...

...am back in the Shaman and I feel it when the Killen crumbles back into the soil from whence it came. Sadness and guilt wash over me. The relationship with the Killen is complicated; a part of the Shaman animates the Killen and so it is almost like losing a child. But the Killen is not a child. There is no innocence in that demonic being, but the Shaman senses that there is maybe a childish bewilderment about its own state of being, and so, he cannot escape the guilt he feels.

Like any child of man, does the Killen seek the answers to its existence?

For a season, there is peace for the People and no stranger strays too deeply into the Pine Barrens; the news of the Killen must be widespread and frightening. Just as the Shaman wanted. Then comes a day when a man rides in on horseback and declares to the People's Chief that the government wants to put a road through this part of the Barrens, so that the wealthy of Philadelphia might be able to access the glittering shorelines of New Jersey for trade and also for recreation.

The Shaman stands by the Chief and puts a restraining hand on his arm. With his eyes alone, he bids the Chief agree...agree to what the white man wants and send him on his way. The People have an answer to the interlopers.

A week more and they have readied themselves. They have gathered the materials necessary and consecrated the ground...the Shaman is ready to call the demon.

The ritual is the same as before; in my curled hand lie the sparse beginnings of the Killen, requiring only the ritual to bring it forth. I breathe in the life force of the People collected before me and hold it in my lungs until I feel it beat and stir in the confined space. I purse my lips to my hand and breathe out slowly, the heat and moisture warming my aching, ancient old joints.

I draw another breath from the circle before me, but this time there is an odd hitch...as I breathe out into my palm I realize the air from my lungs has an odd flavor, a strange hint of foreign...my eyes lift to the circle of the People and I see the white lawman, sitting on his horse just past the firelight...and I want to pull the breath back, I want to throw the dirt in my hand in a wide scatter so that it could never coa-

lesce, but it is too late.

The sand and sticks begin their shifting and I lay it before me, fear and anguish beating my old, old heart. I lift my face and cry out, "aaaaaaaaaahhhhh," as I feel a tearing, seizing in my chest and down my arm. The People follow my lead with their own cry and I want to stop them; this demon is not of the People alone, but it is too late. There is a feeling like lightning in my chest, a heat that radiates through my back and then the pain is everything. I fall forward just as the Killen is sitting up and it catches me in its brand new arms. I stare into the dead onyx orbs of its eyes and watch as its mouth gapes open.

"faaaaaaaaa..." it says and its voice is nothing more than dark wind through a desolate forest but I hear what it intends to say: father. There is an odd fleck in one of its eyes, I squint and try to pull myself closer, even as I feel death coming to claim me. In the deep black of the Killen's stone eye there is a flash of blue; the pale color of the white man's eyes and I try to cry out, to warn the People, but then a weight closes my eyes and I am...

...nothing there is nothing am I dying am I dead did I die with the old Indian, but...

... I'm not dead, I'm here, not there; I am not dead," I say and to my own ears, my voice is muzzy and weak. I have a distinct sense of surfacing. Breaking through black waves into warmth and light. I can't get my eyes to open.

"JD," True says; I'm relieved that it's True's voice and her hands are on my shoulders, shaking me. I don't know what I was expecting. Saint Peter, maybe. "Please JD, please wake up. JD? Wake up, please." Her voice has a tired note as though she has repeated these words over and over.

How long have I been out? I open my eyes to morning sun glittering weakly through the pines. Still morning–not too long, then.

True is staring down at me, tears on her cheeks. Roger stands over her, but he's faced away. What is Roger looking at?

"Can we get him up? I think I see something coming," Roger says. His voice holds a bright thread of barely controlled panic but there's something else there, too. Anticipation?

"I'm okay, I can get up," I say and True stands, gripping my hands and pulling me up with her. I am immediately dizzy and red dots swarm my vision. "Whoa."

Roger's arm is around my back, steadying me and urging me forward. I see where he wants to go...no way. I'm not going in that hovel. Not after what I just saw. I plant my feet and shake my head, but that only increases the dizziness.

"No. No way. It'll kill me," I tell them. True looks worriedly to Roger, but he never hesitates in his insistence on moving me forward. He's determined to get us into that cabin. Obviously, he's very worried to be caught out here with the Killen.

"Come on," Roger says, "Just don't touch anything once we're in there. We can't stay out here. They're coming."

That gets me going. I don't want to die in a crazy vision, but I also don't want a Killen to get me. The brief time I spent as a Killen in my vision is enough for one lifetime, thank you very much.

The door doesn't open so much as it kind of collapses inward, the original wood so enrobed in soft moss that it has become spongy. It's difficult to say what holds it together. Unless it's actually the moss itself binding it, acting like a thick green skin.

Inside seems only a darker version of outside. If there had ever been a floor, it's gone now and the ground is soft and pliable; it's almost like walking on a dirt-encrusted mattress. Vines seem to be the only things keeping the walls upright and a constellation of holes in the roof allow pencil-thin beams of light to shine down. Dust dances in and out of the beams, sparkling darkly. It's cooler in here but the air smells like dirt. It is a dank, basement smell. Or maybe it's the smell of a graveyard.

I keep my hands tucked tight in my armpits. No way do I want to touch anything in here.

Roger manhandles the door back into place and then rubs his hands on his pants, coming back to the center of the room. True and I stand close together, trying to see through the bright beams of light. They look almost solid in the gloom, like prison bars.

The walls are mottled gray and green and it's hard to see if they are log or boards or what. The back wall is in deep shadow and it's impossible to see anything back there.

Roger goes to one of the side windows and looks out, staying well back. True takes the window next to him.

I glance at the back wall again. It's coming a little clearer as my eyes adjust. It looks like it's the same gray green as the side walls, but there's something about it. I take a step closer, squinting...

"Do you see anything?"

I jump and turn at True's question, but she's directing it to Roger. He shakes his head and sighs. It is a strange sigh, full of longing and anticipation. "I don't see them, but I know they're nearby. I can feel them."

True shoots me a look of confusion, and I shrug my shoulders. He can't mean it like I would have meant it. Roger isn't a psychic.

"Roger, what do you mean 'you can feel them'?" True asks.

He glances at her and a flash of light from one of the holes in the roof illuminates his face for a brief second. He looks dazed, almost surprised at her question.

"I can feel them," he says again, and his voice is dazed, too.

"Roger," True says, stepping forward to try and see him more clearly, "What do you mean you can feel them? I don't understand."

He tilts his head and there is something odd, alien, in his movements. His face is entirely in shadow now but his head and shoulders are outlined in a strong backlight. True looks small and vulnerable standing in front of him. I have a surge of uneasiness and I take a step forward, wanting to put myself between them.

His arm lifts and I think he's going to strike True, but instead he points past her, to the back wall. "They brought me this," he says. His head is still tilted, his face in shadow.

I turn and realize that my eyes have adjusted to the darkness. I can see the back wall.

Trooper Stiles is tied to it, his feet dangling three feet from the floor. His arms are spread wide and tied at the wrists. His shirt has been removed and his head is hanging onto his bare chest.

There is a rustling from each back corner and the sound sends a shiver up my spine. It is a desolate sound, like wind through treetops on a cold and bleak winter day. It is a lonely, inhuman sound.

The Killen are here.

Christine Dougherty

-*19*-

True and I sit shoulder to shoulder against the wall under the windows. We each have had our hands tied together behind our backs. I strain to keep mine up and off the floor and my biceps and shoulders are paying the price, but I don't think I could have sat here touching the wall or floor of this cabin again. I know enough. Too much.

Roger had tied our hands as the two Killen stood behind and watched with empty, unnerving patience. True had pleaded with him and then raged at him, but his eyes had stayed remote and uncaring. Now he stands between the Killen before Stiles' body and they sway together, but just slightly. There is going to be a ritual and they are just getting warmed up.

True leans closer to me. Her eyes are red from anger and tears. "Do you know what's going on? What's happened to Roger?"

I nod, not taking my eyes from the trio before Stiles. Although it's still dark in this cabin, the Killen are startling to look at.

"I think so...most of it, anyway," I whisper. "The Lenni-Lenape Indians used to live in the Pine Barrens way back before white settlers came here. But when they did come, they caused a lot of problems for the Lenni...they wanted to take all their land and build roads and clear the Barrens to plant fields and build their homesteads. Everything that was happening all over the United States was happening here, too, you know? In other words, the original People were getting the short end of the stick.

"The Lenni-Lenape had a very strong Medicine man. Very old and accomplished. He was the one who summoned the first Killen to protect the woods from the intruders. The Killen was essentially a pile of consecrated sticks and dirt that the Medicine man used to hold the spirit of the People, his being the biggest 'piece' breathed into the creature. The Killen was his creation, his baby, but in another sense, it belonged to the entire tribe.

"It worked for a long time…until there were all sorts of legends about a creature that haunted the Barrens and people were afraid to come out here; they were even afraid to travel through here. That's probably where the Jersey Devil myth came from.

"But then something went wrong.

"The Medicine man died while conjuring the final Killen and where it would normally only have a small piece of the Medicine man's life force, that last Killen had it all. And it was a very strong life force; it made the Killen unusually strong, too. But that's not the only thing that went wrong.

"When he took the People's essence and put it in the Killen, that was what protected them. The Killen wouldn't harm what he recognized as his own kind...at least, that was what they thought. But that last time, a white man–a lawman–had come into the circle of the People without the Medicine man's knowledge. A small bit of that man ended up in the Killen, too."

The trio in front of Stiles is swaying harder. Roger is flanked by the two Killen. They are tall and horribly misshapen. Big heads, sloping shoulders. Their arms end in rough hands with claws of a yellowish dirty brown.

"Why are there two now?" True asks. "I thought there was just one in your vision."

I nod. "There was just one. But it was very strong, strong enough to hold itself together. I think it made more like itself."

"But how? Out of what? Wouldn't it need more...life force or whatever? Where would it have gotten more life force? Unless..."

I look at her and I know what she's thinking. Her face has flown open in shocked anger. I shouldn't be surprised that even now she is angrier than she is scared. I think briefly of the visions I had of her. Her whole young life was a trial by fire. And she certainly has come out the other side tempered and strong.

I'm not happy to be in this situation, but one thing I am happy about is that it is True next to me. Who knows? We might have a chance, yet.

"You're right, I think...the first one must have started turning on the People...using them for their life forces, making new Killen. Maybe it was even lonely. I don't know. When I was...in it...experiencing everything it had experienced...all I felt was rage and need. It wanted to be human; maybe it still wants it. It doesn't realize it's impossible."

"How have they taken over Roger? That's what they've done, isn't it? Is it some kind of mind control or something?"

I shake my head. "I don't think so, not really. Remember how you told me Roger has Indian blood? My best guess is that he's descended from the Lenni-Lenape. He's just finally come home."

A loud moan startles me, and I turn to the trio, thinking their ritual has escalated. But they still sway in slow time. Then another movement catches my eye.

Stiles' head comes up and he groans.

Adrenalin slams sickly into my system revving my heart. My stomach sours with fear for Stiles' safety, but there is also a small kick of hope.

"Look," I whisper to True, and she follows the direction of my gaze. She gasps, but it's a small, controlled intake of breath.

"He's awake," she says, and I hear the same hope in her voice that I feel warming my chest.

But it's short-lived because the Killen reaches forward and with it's thick, yellowish claws it draws four lines down the right side of Stiles' face. The lines quickly fill with blood that looks almost black in the gloom and now the Killen's claws travel on, tearing the same four lines down Stiles' neck and continuing down his chest. Stiles' head lifts again and he moans in pain, grimacing.

"Stop it, leave him alone!" True says, but the Killen never hesitates. "Leave him alone!" True's voice teeters on the edge between panic and rage and tears sparkle in her eyes. I struggle with the bindings on my wrists; they are thick, pliable vines and very strong. True is rubbing her hands rapidly back and forth, over and over each other in a desperate attempt to loosen them from the vines. Her wrists are red and beginning to bead with blood where they abrade her skin.

A high, insectile whine begins, and I assume it is an escalation in the ritual and I struggle harder. I brace myself against the cabin wall and try to push up, but it's impossible with my feet and legs out straight in front of me.

Stiles lets out a small, tired bellow. He sounds like a man struggling to wake from a nightmare. The Killen has begun to tear matching fissures down the other side of his face. True's struggles intensify in answer to Stiles' cries.

The whining, buzzing sound increases in volume. True has rolled onto her side and is trying to bring her hands under her feet. "Stay still," I say and turn over, my back to hers. "Can you–?"

I don't even get a chance to finish my question before her

hands are on mine, her fingers walking over the knots, deciphering. The whine is now almost entirely a buzz, and I look at the Killen as True starts to pick at the vines.

They are still swaying, intent upon their task. Roger lifts a knife and the Killen turn to track it with their dead black eyes. He holds it over his head with both hands, two feet from Stiles' defenseless chest. They stop swaying. Roger's head tilts and he turns abruptly. His eyes go first to True and I and my first thought is that he's going to kill us for trying to untie our hands. But then his gaze travels past us and to the window. That's when I realize the noise–the humming whine–isn't coming from the Killen; it's coming from outside.

True's hands have stilled and I strain my head back to see her. Her gaze, too, is trained on the window above, though she can't possibly see out. Then she rolls half over until she can see me.

"Quads," she says and a large, relieved grin spreads across her features.

Quads? What the heck are quads?

The sound outside clarifies and I realize it's the sound of small, straining engines. Now I know what True meant by quads…it's four wheelers, at least three of them by the sound. They are right outside the cabin.

There's another low, rustling from the back and I turn just in time to see Roger squeezing through an opening in the corner. The Killen must have already squeezed out to escape into the woods.

"JD? Are you in there?" A voice calls from outside, and it's a split second before I recognize it–Dex. Saving me again.

"Yes! We're here!" True says and her voice is triumphant. "Help us! We're in here!"

The moss-covered front door is pushed roughly open and it collapses inward in a heap. Dex is the first through, followed by two soldiers in uniform.

Soldiers?

I'm always happy to see Dex, but this time is also filled with a relief so great that I feel tears lining up in the back of my throat, tightening it. I can't say anything.

He squints into the gloom and spots us. He's next to me in a flash, kneeling down and tearing at the vines on my wrists.

"What happened?" He says, and his voice is filled with relief and anger in equal measure.

"Dex, you have to help Stiles, he–"

But one of the soldiers has already found him and he cuts Stiles down, catching him before he falls to the floor. Stiles groans again.

"What happened here?" the soldier says. "I've got you. Hang in there, buddy."

"You have to get him out. Before they come back." I hear the hysteria lacing my voice and realize right away that it's a mistake. The soldier untying True squints at me suspiciously.

"Before who comes back?"

Dex has untied the vines and he pulls me up and into a hug. Crushes me, actually. I can't breathe much less answer the soldier. It really is good to see Dex.

True is sitting against the wall. "The Killen. Before the Killen come back. They're monsters. They got Roger."

A look passes between the soldier helping her and the soldier at Stiles' side. "What do you mean 'they got Roger'?"

"Because of his blood, his Indian blood. They think he's their leader. But they might kill him. For his life force. JD? Tell them what you saw. Tell them about the sticks and the dirt and the Medicine man."

Another look passes between the soldiers. Raised eyebrows from the one and the hint of a cynical grin from the other.

Oh, crap.

***

"How did you find us?" I hadn't thought to ask this in the rush of everything going on. Dex is watching one of the quads as it disappears into the woods. The one driving Stiles to safety. The quads are big, two or even three person vehicles and they are painted in green and gray camouflage. The soldiers will have Stiles to the base hospital in no time. He'll be okay.

Dex turns to me.

"Your phone. The GPS on it. The soldiers had a tracking device that…well, it worked, if only intermittently. We'd have been here sooner if…" He trails off. "I contacted the base when we were cut off. I have a few friends there." Dex has friends everywhere; important friends who owe him favors. He smiles at me. "How were the woods? Fun?"

I nod and laugh shakily. "Yeah. Tons of fun. Wish I didn't have to leave." I glance at the two remaining quads. I am just about drooling in anticipation. I've never wanted anything as much as I've wanted to get myself out of the Pine Barrens. My room flashes into my mind: small, cozy, and familiar. Every inch of it a known quantity. Oh, man, I really can't wait to get home.

True touches my arm.

"What are we going to do about Roger? And Pepper?"

"The soldier will…he'll find…" But I know it's no use and I feel a weight settle around me. When True had asked the soldiers to go after Roger and the Killen and pointed out the direction they must have gone when they left the cabin, they'd more or less reassured her that they would do everything they could. But they hadn't even looked around. Of course, their main concern was getting Stiles on a quad and out, but that was done now. Stiles was on his way to safety. A sharp stick of jealousy poked me in the chest. Somehow I knew that I wasn't going to get out that easily.

I look into True's eyes. She is calm and sure and just slightly impatient. I can read what she wants us to do. She wants us to go after Roger. I open my mouth to tell her 'no, no way' but close it again before saying anything. She is so strong, so brave. I'd never be as brave as this girl.

"You can track them," she says, lowering her voice, but the remaining soldier overhears anyway.

"No. Out of the question. I'm getting the three of you out of here, then I'll come back with a squad and look for the other Ranger."

I don't like how he refers to Roger as 'the other Ranger'…it has a shrinking, dehumanizing effect.

But I nod. "Fine with me. The sooner I get out of here the better. I've had enough of pine trees to last me a lifetime." I walk to Dex's side, leaving True to stand alone near the cabin. It nearly breaks my heart, and it takes every ounce of my will to turn my back on her.

I don't look, but I can sense her shocked, hurt expression.

The soldier nods and turns to his quad.

Dex is looking at me askance and I see a question in his eyes. He knows me so well. There is no question that he is the father I never had. I nod slightly, just enough for his eyes alone. He raises his eyebrows: you're sure?

I nod again and he shakes his head the smallest bit and a wry grin appears at the corner of his mouth. "Ah, love," he says only loud enough for me to hear. I am gratified that he has understood the situation so completely.

"Private," Dex says, walking to the soldier. "What about that knife?"

The soldier turns. "What knife is that, Mr. Hammond?"

Dex puts a hand on the soldier's shoulder and begins to lead him to the cabin. "That Ranger had a knife, according to the kids." I glance at True, and she flushes a deep, angry red at Dex's use of the word 'kids' but she doesn't speak, merely clenches her jaw. She's planning on bolting once Dex and the soldier are in the cabin; I can see it in her face and in her tense posture. I want to smile but I can't, not yet.

"I think it's important that we find it. The State Troopers are going to want to examine it and also…" His voice trails away as they enter the cabin.

True walks swiftly and silently past the cabin door, angling toward the quads. She's going to commandeer one and ride after Roger. But the soldier will be out in a flash if he hears the engine kick over.

"True, don't," I say, my voice quiet. I step toward her and put a hand on her arm.

Her jaw clenches again. "JD, I have to. I know you're scared. I know you want to go back. That's okay, it is. But I can't. I can't do it. I have to help Roger." Her hand is on the ignition and I put my hand over hers.

"Not like this," I say, "True, look at me."

She hesitates, and then looks. Her eyes are ringed dark

with fear and exhaustion and an ass-busting determination that is the bedrock, the core, of her personality. I love her. I really do.

"Look over my shoulder," I say, and confusion clouds her features, but she looks. "She's in the woods at about three o'clock." True's wonderful, mysterious, beautiful, intelligent, determined black eyes shift and then they open wide. "She'll be a lot quieter than a quad, too."

"Pepper," she says, her voice a reverential whisper. Then her eyes come back to mine. "You knew she was there? You planned this all along?"

I nod. "From the time we came out of the cabin and I spotted her standing out there. It's like she's counting on us." I grab True's hand. "Let's not keep her…

…*a warm pulse of love comes over me. I am in a small, desolate room. There is a crib but it holds only a bare mattress and one twisted blanket. A little girl, maybe eighteen months old, with dark hair and darker eyes is pushed against the bars of the crib and she reaches for me with grubby little fingers. Her tiny face is lit with a smile in spite of the knotted bruise on her forehead. She is reaching for me and she laughs…*

…waiting," I finish and stumble a little.

"JD?" True says, "Are you okay?"

I look into her eyes one more time then I pull her to me and kiss her.

My first kiss. It's amazing.

I feel her smile against my lips as we part.

"I love you," I say.

She nods. Then she's pulling me past the cabin toward Pepper. "I love you, too. I feel like I always have." She glances at me and her gaze is both puzzled and joyous.

I nod. "Let's go get Roger."

We trek through the woods as quickly as is prudent. We don't want to alert the soldier to our departure, but at the same time, we need to be far enough away so that when they emerge from the cabin, we're out of view.

I can only imagine what Dex is saying to the soldier to keep him occupied. I send Dex a brief, mental thank you. He can't hear me, but I choose to think that he can sense it all the same.

We close in on Pepper and she stands still at our approach.

"Good girl," True says, throwing her arms around Pepper's neck. The horse nods her head up and down as if in agreement. Or maybe it's just impatience, because next she snorts at me.

"Let's go," I say and True swings gracefully up and onto Pepper's back. It's a little more of a struggle for me–I've never been on a horse. But then I'm up and True and I crouch low over Pepper's neck, my arms around True's waist, and True turns her away from the cabin. Pepper begins a rough, jerky trot that shakes my insides like a funhouse ride.

People do this on purpose? I think, even as my head is being snapped up and down and I am being repeatedly slammed into True's back. Although I have to admit, that part wasn't so bad.

Once we're clear of the cabin, True sits upright and I do, too. But I don't take my arms from around her waist. Opportunistic? Guilty as charged.

She's scanning the ground to the left and right, and I ask her what she's looking for.

"A piece of one of those things, one of the Killen. You're going to read it. Find out where they've gone."

I swallow. "I can try. But it doesn't always work the way I want it to. And I've never been able to see into the future or anything." I would do anything for True. But I can't do what I can't do. Even wishing won't make it so.

She nods, not taking her gaze from the trail. "I know that. But can you scan its memories? See if there's anywhere they go on a regular basis?"

"I think that cabin might have been it," I tell her. "It was creepy enough."

"Maybe, but maybe not. That was a settler's cabin, not an Indian's. I think they took Stiles there because it was close and it was easy and because we'd go into it without a fight. I think they would actually live somewhere they were more comfortable."

I shake my head, not in denial but in surprise. "What makes you think all those things?"

She glances back and her face is somber.

"I'm American Indian, too, JD," she says, returning her gaze to the trail. "It could as easily been me as Roger."

I'm surprised and–I have to admit it–more than a little apprehensive. What if the Killen can get into True's thoughts somehow? Control her the way they seem to be controlling Roger? But there are so many variables…I've no way of knowing if they were able to get Roger because he's part Indian or if it's because he's part Indian *coupled with* his immersion in the culture and his obvious sympathies in that direction.

It's possible that I'm just blinded by love, but my instinct is that True is a stronger person than Roger–that she is truer to herself, if you get what I'm saying.

***

It's hot again. We've been on the trail for about a half an hour and it must be close to noon. We heard the distant whine of the quads about fifteen minutes ago. We'd stopped, listening, but they'd gotten quieter as they went away.

A pit had formed in my stomach as the sound disappeared, and the oppressive silence of the Pine Barrens seemed to close in around me like heavy, crevice-filling foam. We're on our own, now, no matter what happens, because I had deliberately left my phone back at the cabin.

We'd dismounted from Pepper both to give her a break and so True could scan the ground more closely. She'd picked up different bent sticks and mangled twigs and handed them to me with a question in her eyes. Nothing had given me any kind of vision, not even a twinge. Either these weren't bits of the Killen or I'd already developed a defensive immunity to them.

True hands me another stick and I run it through my fingers, hand-to-hand and then grasp it tightly. I don't need to do that. If I were going to get a vision, I'd have had it already. The visions either are or they aren't…no coaxing on my part would change that. I hate to admit this, but I just didn't want True to think I wasn't trying.

"No, I'm not getting anything. Are you still sure they came this way?" I glance around. Nothing looks disturbed and everything looks disturbed–it's the woods; it's the nature of nature. I don't know what she's been looking at this whole time.

True nods and points. "See this?" I follow the direction of her finger to a blueberry bush and there's a small branch bent and broken about ten inches from the ground.

I nod.

"Yeah, I see it but anything could have broken that twig. A deer or even a rabbit…what makes you think this is their trail?"

I catch a ghost of smile crossing her lips. "You have to unfocus," she says. "Unfocus your eyes. If you're looking at each thing in the specific, you'll never see it, but if you look at it as a whole, it comes clear."

"I don't understand...show me."

"Here," she says and steps toward me. "Close your eyes."

I close them and then her hands are on my arms and she turns me in a half circle. "Keep them closed until I say and when you open them, try and stay unfocused. Try to see everything at once...nothing in particular."

I nod my head and then her hands leave my arms.

"Open your eyes."

I do and the first thing that happens is my eyes try and focus on what is about ten feet from me–a section of woods we've just come through. I relax and let them go unfocused, tilting my head back slightly. When I do that...it's weird, it's almost like having one of the visions. Everything gets very soft. Sun dappled leaves develop flaring blooms of yellow and green and even white. The hard tree trunks fuzz at the edges and lighten and begin to disappear into the sea of branches and then the branches, too, begin to intermingle to the point where everything looks like camouflage.

Once the woods have flattened themselves I can see a hole–that's the only way I can describe it–where we have come through. Pepper, especially, has left a wide swath of minute destruction starting from the divots in the sand from her hooves and reaching four to five feet high where her shoulders have bent branches. Pine needles, blueberries, and small leaves litter the trail...everything that our passage has shaken loose.

I turn to True, amazed. At first, she is a soft blend of colors, then I allow my eyes to do their job and her face comes into sharp focus.

"That's how you've been doing that this whole time?" I ask.

"Yes and no. I switch back and forth to make sure we're still on their trail but still check the details as we go along."

I look in the direction we've been heading. "Let me try it again." I let my gaze soften and tilt my head back just a little and I see the hole–or tunnel, actually–that True has been leading us through. It's so obvious once you see it. I'm amazed, but as I turn to ask True a question, a dark area registers in my vision. My eyes focus but then I force them to relax again. I scan back and forth, looking for the anomaly. True must not have seen it because she was only looking ahead, following the trail of the Killen and Roger.

"What did you see?" she asks.

"I'm not sure, it was just this black hole or a mass of some kind but..." I trail off, concentrating. Then I see it. A shiver of undefined origin starts at the top of my spine and rides it like a ramshackle slide to the bottom. I focus my eyes and although the woods become defined, the black shape doesn't really change. It is roughly triangular with a wide, grounded base tapering to a point as it rises into the air. It is about a third to half as tall as the pines, so about twenty-five to thirty feet high.

It looks wrong in a way I can't explain but True sums it up with a handful of words.

"That shouldn't be there," she says in a whisper.

***

Unlike a cabin forged from the natural things that surround it or a teepee that mimics the soft textures and colors of the landscape, this structure is a deep, unnatural black. Charred, burned, blackened tree trunks with the limbs removed and tapering from base to tip as though each had been turned on a giant's lathe have been stacked in a cylinder with a diameter at the base that looks to be about fifty feet. The points of these barely recognizable trees are gathered together at the top, forming one tall axis. The only thing that seems to hold them up is their intertwined weight. It looks like the biggest, nastiest, weirdest bird's nest in the history of the planet, the hellish lair of a pterodactyl from the netherworld.

There is one access space—a rough doorway—where no trees have been stacked, and it, too, tapers from a base about four feet wide to an inverted v that is about ten feet from the ground. I can't see anything through that black hole to the depths inside.

This structure looks like an abode of the damned.

If the Killen live here, and I sense that they do, then it *is* an abode of the damned. I don't know if there is a creature (or non-creature as the case may be) that lives a colder, less *felt* existence than the Killen.

The gaping black hole in the center of the structure makes me more and more uneasy the longer I stare into it. I can feel the tension in Pepper's body where my hand rests on her side. I wonder if True is as freaked out as I am and I look past Pepper to where True kneels, staring intently at the monstrous tangle of wood. Her expression is calm but intent. She glances at me and gives me a brief smile. I'm amazed all over again by her inherent strength and fearlessness. I wonder about her terrible childhood and I can't wait to ask her about it. I especially want to ask her why her baby self seems to see me in the visions.

A scrim of blueberry bushes and mountain laurel are all that separates us from that black opening. Anything could come out at any second and we've no weapons of any kind. Then I think of something. I lean forward again until True is in my sightline.

"Fire," I say, and she looks at me and shakes her head in confusion. "We could use fire. As a weapon against the Killen. Don't you think so? They're mostly made of sticks and what not. They'd go up in a second."

She nods, considering the idea, liking it. Then her features cloud. "But what about Roger? Fire would kill him."

Somehow I'd forgotten about that part. Will he fight us every step of the way? Even if we can destroy the Killen, would Roger magically return to normal? I don't feel like anything is guaranteed right now. And I don't want to fight Roger.

"If we separate them somehow? Get Roger away from them and then keep him away while we destroy the Killen?" she says. There is a considering light in her eyes. I don't know what she is thinking...but I know it's something I'm not going to like.

"We could try, but..." I shake my head. "But we don't have a fast way to make fire. Unless you can do the stick rubbing together thing. Even if you can, I get the impression that would take a little while."

True fishes in her pocket. She pulls out a battered, flip-top lighter. There's a red cross on the side. "I'm always prepared," she says with a hint of a grin. She pops the top and thumbs the wheel and a gorgeous blue flame springs to life. A whiff of the butane wafts across to me and Pepper snorts...she must have smelled it, too. Or maybe the fire makes her nervous. Horses have a phobia or something about fire, right?

"That's perfect. Now we just have to get Roger to come

out and then we can light the whole thing up," I say. "Killen and all."

But True is shaking her head. "I don't think it's going to work like that. Those trees were burned once already and without some kind of incendiary agent, it would be very difficult to get them going again. Even if we stacked kindling all around the bottom, it would still take hours for the flames to get high enough and hot enough to get through to the burnable wood on those trees. No…we'll have to get a flame right onto the Killen."

This means one or both of us will have to be in reaching distance of those things, and I don't think they'd just stand still and let us light them up; not when they could reach out with those long, frighteningly sharp claws and…oh, man, this doesn't sound like a good idea. Plus, we'll still have Roger to contend with more likely than not. I saw the drugged, determined look on his face when he held the knife up to Stiles. He's not going to go any easier on us.

All this goes through my head in a flash and I'm about to tell True all the reasons we can't go with her plan, but before I get the chance, she says, "Let's lead Pepper a little further back. I don't want her near any of this and I don't want those things to get her."

I nod, resigned. *I've come this far,* I think, *may as well see it through to the end.* Even as I have this thought, I am amazed by it. Is this really me? My room at the hospital seems far away and almost…unreal. I wonder–if I get out of this–whether the comfort of those close quarters might from now on feel a little more like confinement. After an adventure like this, will my life change? I think it might. A hot thrill of adrenaline courses through me and I stand.

True and I lead Pepper back through the woods and loop her reins over a low branch. She'll be able to pull away if anything scares her. Then we head back to the structure.

"I think we should try and lure them out," True says. Fine with me…I've no driving desire to go exploring in that black nightmare of a cavern. "If we can get Roger to separate from the Killen, then we'll be in good shape. Maybe I can even reason with him. Maybe the Killen only have a limited hold on him."

I nod. "Let's make torches first. If we use a heavy branch and bundle some of these dry leaves and grasses at the end, it should burn pretty well. If you can jam a torch right down into the Killen, I bet it would go up like a match."

"Okay, yeah, that's a good idea. How many were there in total? We should make at least that many torches." She squats and begins to draw together piles of kindling then she pulls handfuls of long, dried grass that can be used to tie the smaller sticks and leaves to the ends of the torches. I squat next to her. We both have our backs to the structure. I pull over some semi-straight sticks–bigger ones that we can use as the handles.

"At least the two, but there might be more. If I count back…"

It's fun discussing strategy with True. I feel like a kid playing war. Our plan, vague as it is, seems foolproof to me. If this were a movie, then we're obviously the spunky good guys who will have a handy win and then a long, much deserved kiss. Perhaps even as we stand triumphantly over the charred remains of a Killen.

Then I am forcibly reminded that this isn't a movie.

A hot line of pain imprints down my back like a lash whip and I bow sharply forward away from the searing sting. Unable to stand from my ungainly crouching bow, I'm tumbled forward, my face connecting painfully with the sand.

True cries out, and I turn my head in time to see her being dragged away between two Killen. She kicks and struggles. There's a lot of blood on her face. I push myself upright but am then shoved rudely down again. I feel like I've been struck with a tree branch, and in a way, I guess that's what happened. I roll, desperate to get away. As my back connects with the rasping sand, another wave of pain shoots through me. The cuts must be numerous and pretty deep.

A Killen stands over me. It raises its limb-like arm to deliver another blow.

Its eyes are soulless flat black pieces of chipped shale. Its head is enormous and terribly misshapen atop its small, sloped shoulders…it looks like a caricature or badly made doll. Its body is ragged and ravaged looking; it looks as though it's lost at least a third of its mass and even as it stands over me, a section roughly the size of my hand made of sand, twigs and pine needles loosens and cascades to the forest floor.

It is literally falling apart in front of me.

It crosses my mind that they are desperate for more of the energy that animates them; that keeps them intact.

True.

Ignoring the fresh pain in my back, I kick out reflexively and my boots connect with the Killen's legs. There is a sharp snap as one of the main supports in its legs breaks and it lurches sideways. It swipes at me but misses. A light pattering of sand stings my cheek. I kick out again, pressing my advantage but my feet pass through nothing as the Killen collapses backward into the brush. It is something like watching a dried up Christmas tree crumbling in on itself.

I gain my feet and scramble after True. Her legs are disappearing into the black opening. An icy feeling seizes my brain–I don't want to go into that nightmare teepee. I don't want to go anywhere near it. The third Killen reappears at the edge of the brush line, seeming to reform as it shuffles forward. It limps and stumbles into the doorway after True.

My legs start to move me toward the structure. My brain is screaming at my legs to *stop, stop, that way is dangerous, that way is death!* But my legs, I guess, are braver than they are smart and in three seconds they carry me to the dark threshold.

I hesitate at the entrance, my brain demanding that my legs turn me around and run, and my legs stubbornly itching to move me forward into the teepee. Maybe my brain is going to win this fight or flight impasse and send me tearing off into the woods–the longer I stand here, the more it seems like the choice I am about to make. Then a faint, odd echo clangs into my head–it's there and gone in a flash: *down, look down, please, JD, look down, look down, look*…the brief echo was True's voice. How can she be in my head? I look down.

Her lighter glints up at me from the dirt.

She must have somehow scrambled it from her pocket and dropped it here for me to find. I bend to retrieve it and rub my thumb over the red cross. A brief flash of panic and anger–True's–flows into my mind but along with it comes a warm pulse of love. Her love for me.

Finally, finally my brain picks up the rally cry my legs have been trying to make all along and a calming sense of courage comes over me.

I walk into the black.

-20-

The light from outside seems almost magically cut off at the entrance; I can't see anything. I wave my hand in front of my eyes...I feel the slight breeze but my hand doesn't materialize. I look back and the entrance is still illuminated, but the light seems unable to penetrate the inky dark. It is much cooler in here, but carries the feeling of dank, fetid air too long in one place...in other words, it's far from refreshing.

I stand very still and listen until I can almost feel the strain in my ears. Nothing. No sounds at all. From the outside, it looks like this should be a room roughly fifty feet in diameter. If True, Roger and the Killen were here, then I'd hear them. There's no way they'd all be this quiet.

I consider the lighter but don't want to give myself away. Instead, I take a cautious step forward. Then another. I look back over my shoulder and the doorway is a bright triangle...but it looks about twice as far away as it should. Is this space getting bigger? Or am I just freaking myself out? I hope for the latter and take a deep breath. And another step forward.

A sudden, light breeze against the underside of my chin startles me into taking a shuffling step back, and I instinctively flick the wheel on the lighter, bringing the warm flame to life. As my eyes adjust, I realize I'm at the edge of what appears to be a large pit. One more step and I would have tumbled all the way to…well, wherever this hole goes.

My legs begin to shake in reaction, and I remind them that they wanted to come here in the first place and they had better get tough.

Now that I have the lighter lit, I may as well check the place out. It's obvious that no one is here. I glance up, but where the trees come together, it's too high for the lighter's light to penetrate. I turn in a slow circle, illuminating the walls–they look even blacker on the inside than they had on the outside–but beyond that, are featureless. I look back into the hole in the floor. I hadn't seen it at first, but at second glance, there is a ladder leaned against one side. It's made of intertwined limbs and looks less than stable, of course. I kneel and reach down, trying to see if the light will reach a floor down there…it doesn't. Of course.

I realize I won't be able to climb down and use the lighter at the same time.

I'll have to navigate that rickety ladder in the pitch black. Of course!

***

I try to keep a running total of rungs as I descend, but I lose track quickly as the ladder sways and creaks and seems about to buckle under my weight. I can't be very far down, maybe ten or fifteen feet, but it feels like I've been on this ladder forever. Visions bump around the edges of my mind like big fish in cloudy water but I hold them at bay. I can't force a vision to appear, but I can sometimes concentrate on holding them off; the last thing I want is a blast from the Killen's nightmare existence. I feel a panic wave trying to wring itself up through my guts and I conjure a picture of True. That stems the tide nicely. Plus, it's also just good to picture her face.

I grip the ladder more tightly with my right hand and flick the lighter awake with my left. I look over my shoulder and down. I see a dirt floor. It was only just out of the lighter's reach from the edge, then. It gives me renewed energy, and I pocket the lighter and finish the climb down.

It's even colder at the bottom of the shaft and there's a steady breeze; it's almost refreshing compared to the rank air of the teepee. I hear sounds, faint and far off. I flick the lighter open, guarding the flame with my hand. To my surprise, I am looking into what appears to be a cave entrance. It's a rocky semi-circle about twelve feet high and fifteen or so wide. The breeze is flowing directly from the cave mouth and I cock my head and listen intently.

Barely, just barely, I hear True's voice, but I can't make out the words. Her tone is high, strident, panicked. My stomach bumps into my heart, making it stumble for a few beats, then it smoothes out, even though my stomach still seems to be fighting for space in my chest. I have to get to her now.

I enter the tunnel, keeping my hand around the flame. I have enough light to move steadily forward, but hopefully not enough to give away my approach. True's voice continues to rise and now under it, I can hear a low hum; it sound mechanical. Soulless.

I quicken my pace to a trot as my stomach knots and unknots. The humming is part of some ritual, I'm almost sure of it; it's like a clouded memory that I can't quite bring to the fore. Were they humming when they were getting ready to cut Stiles? In my panicked state, I can't remember.

There's a curve in the tunnel and when I get around it, my light seems to jump far ahead of me, glittering on the rock wall. I douse the flame with my free hand. The orange and yellow light on the wall continues to shimmer, and I realize they must be right around the next bend.

True's voice has become low, guttural. I can't tell if she is pleading or scolding. The hum continues unabated.

Staying close to the wall, I slide silently around the last bend. The space opens before me into a large cavern. The walls rise into black invisibility and I become aware of steady dripping. Fifty feet from me, a large fire burns in the center of the cavern. On the far side of it, True is struggling in the grasp of two Killen. They have forced her onto her knees and each has one of her arms. Her face is lit with the flickering flame and it lends a feverish quality to the tableau. Roger is before her, his back to the fire. He is humming and swaying, arms raised above his head. He is holding a long knife.

The humming seems to be at some sort of crescendo, and I think Roger is about to bring the knife down and I shout to distract him. He turns and his face in the firelight is somehow both devilish and blank. I can't see the eyes of the Killen from here, but I register the turn of their heads.

Twin tracks of tears glitter on True's face and her eyes go to mine in shocked surprise. She wasn't expecting me to save her.

"JD, be careful there's–!" Her harsh, despairing voice is cut off as Roger's hand swings down and he slaps her across the cheek, open-handed, sending her head rocking back on her neck.

Every trace of panic and un-sureness leaves my body as rage floods into me, heating me up. Pushing me forward. I hear an inarticulate, warlike cry and realize it is coming from my outraged throat. I run toward Roger, no thought of consequences, my vision clouding at the edges. I feel as though my boots don't even touch the hard, rocky floor.

Roger turns toward me and his face finally registers an emotion: fear.

I will kill him for hitting True.

My eyes have not left Roger's face and a weird wave of relief flies over it and for the briefest second, I think he is coming back to himself...that my charge has made him remember who he is and who's side he should be on.

That's when my lights go out.

***

I come to, lying on my back and disoriented. I try to sit up and a large wallop of pain in my head makes me groan. Plus, there's an area of pressure on my shoulders. I squint my eyes open and the first thing I see is True's face hanging over mine. Firelight glows warmly on the side of her cheek. Small flecks of red glitter and jump like fireworks as she runs a hand through her hair, tucking it behind her ear.

"My hero," she says and bends to kiss me. Even in my dazed state, her kiss seems magical, rejuvenating. Her hand brushes my thigh, right near my…well, you know. I flush with warmth. I appreciate the press of her lips, the wax and wane as she pulls away. She is smiling. I clear my throat. Even that brings fresh pain to my head.

"Did I get them?" It is my hope, but I'm unsure. I can't remember what happened once the rage overtook me. Maybe I Hulked out in some fashion, bringing this whole adventure to a satisfying close. I hoped so. "Did we win?"

Her smile slips, and she glances somewhere over my head. Then she's yanked back and away, and I raise my head enough to see the Killen pulling her by her arms. I struggle to rise, but find I'm being restrained, too. I look up and up, over my head.

The third Killen is holding me in place; its sticking, poking tree and dirt arms are holding my shoulders down. It must have been behind me when I rushed in to save True. On one level, I feel like a jackass for being so easily overcome at the height of my charge. On another level, I hope this sinking embarrassment isn't the last thing I'll feel on this earth.

Roger is above me, hands raised, knife glinting in the same firelight that had lit True's beautiful face. He's humming. And swaying.

Oh, shit.

I try and kick my legs up, but they're being restrained, too. I wrench again, unmindful of the pain in my head. Then I remember the lighter. My hands are free so I scramble my hand into my pocket. No lighter. The other pocket. No lighter there, either. They must have found it or it fell out when I charged.

Either way, it was my last hope and now it's gone.

I get angry all over again.

"Roger, you asshole! Wake the hell up, man! Don't you see what—"

The humming stops and his eyes fly open, but he isn't looking at me; he's looking off into the distant black. He's gone. Long gone. His arms tremble and his body is taut as strung wire. The knife trembles, too, seemingly in sympathy. He's about to plunge that knife right into me so the Killen can have my life force. So they can stop falling apart. Just like they must have killed those kids, Gater and Mindy. And Andrew and Jackson.

Then they'll kill True for hers, too.

The firelight glints wickedly on that vibrating knife-edge. It seems to glow with a life–and a heat–of its own. The brightness blooms to the point where I have to squint my eyes and then I realize the light isn't come from the knife, it's coming from the fire…it must be raging out of control.

I glance at the bonfire behind Roger but it looks the same. Where is the light coming from? The heat?

All at once, I am aware of two things: one of the Killen holding True has burst into flame and…

…*they feel each other, linked, they are linked, like bees in a hive, a hive mind, and the burning the burning is the greatest pain the worst thing ever felt, even worse then the shedding, the crumbling of the form, but worse than the pain of the burning is the sense of the end, the fear, the pathetic terror and the sense of its own soulless existence ending, the end so near, the end is here!*…

I snap forward, given extra strength by my overwhelming desire to break free of that particular vision. I don't want to burn with the Killen.

The one holding me has gone lax. It seems to stare in onyx-eyed, glittering awe at the Killen that is now dancing like an animated torch. The other Killen that had been restraining True is also held in thrall, and I watch as True leans over, extending her arm. The lighter is in her hand. It is lit and she punches her hand deep into the other Killen's middle and it, too, bursts into flame.

A screeching cry of pain rings through the cavern as the two burning Killen jerk wildly about. Whole sections of them break free and lay burning on the ground. The flames eat through them quickly. The first one to be set alight has already begun crumbling in on itself and the second isn't far behind. I scramble up next to True and throw my arms around her. She's trembling and can't seem to take her eyes from the two burning heaps. They still move, but sluggishly, like discorporated phantoms.

"True, we have to get out of here." I take her face in my hands and turn it to me. Her eyes are large and dazed.

"I feel it," she says and her voice is a shaky whisper.

"You feel what?"

"The burning, I feel like I'm burning, too!" Her eyes are wide with panic. She clutches my arms in a too-tight grip and she's right, her hands are hot, I can feel it through my shirt. They're burning up. "I must be one of them, just like Roger...JD, help me, please, I don't want to burn!"

I grasp her hands in mine and she cries out in pain. But I see now. I see why she thinks that she is burning, too. In a way, she is...or, was.

"True, it's okay, you're not one of them. You burned your

hands. That's all. You must have burned them when you put the lighter to them. It's okay, look. You're not burning…you're burned."

She looks at her hands. They're scratched and scorched–it's hard to tell the soot from the blood, especially as the light from the dying Killen recedes–but a shaky smile breaks out across her face. She turns her hands over and over and then she laughs.

The laugh is pretty damn shaky, too.

"I'm okay," she says and looks at me with wonder and relief. "I'm not a Killen…not part of them."

I shake my head and smile. "No, you're not a Killen."

She laughs again. She can't seem to stop looking at her hands.

"We have to get out of here. You ready to go?"

She looks at me and nods. I hug her briefly and stand, pulling her up next to me. Roger and the remaining Killen aren't anywhere in sight, but as the light dies, they could be anywhere. I scan the ground and the lighter glints up at me from where True had been held. I scoop it up and we head back to the tunnel mouth.

I stop at the rocky entrance and True crowds up behind me. I glance over my shoulder into her face.

Amazingly, she seems to have regained most, if not all, of her composure. I smile and she smiles back.

"I wanted to save you," I tell her. "I feel bad that…"

She smiles again and shakes her head. "You did!" she says, but I feel like I see a faint shadow of doubt run through her eyes.

"No. You saved me." I tell her, and she just shakes her head again, but this time she isn't smiling. She brushes past me and into the tunnel.

"Let's go, JD," she says. "I want to see some normal light."

I keep the lighter lit and held high through the tunnel and before long we are at the rickety stick ladder leading up and out. At the sight of it, a shiver of unease runs through me.

"Let me go first," I say and reach around her to put my hand on the ladder, but she's already grasped the rungs further up and has a foot up, too.

"I'll go first," she says and glances back the way we just came. She gives me a brief, embarrassed smile. "Just in case, okay?"

I nod, confused, and step back, holding the lighter steady as she begins her ascent. In case of what? But then it hits me: she means in case there's trouble in the teepee. She's afraid to let me go first in case something goes wrong. Something I won't be able to handle. I feel my face darken in hot shame and I'm glad that the light is dim.

I begin my own one-handed ascent.

No way am I going to be able to woo her now. Now that she thinks I'm a coward. A baby in need of protection. Sud-

denly, my room at the hospital seems more like a sad necessity rather than an eccentric choice.

Mental deficients like me need protection, obviously.

Obviously.

My thoughts remain similarly discouraged throughout the
climb. Even as the ladder creaks and shakes, I'm distracted by
my shame. For about the billionth time, I find myself wishing that my parents had lived and that I'd had a normal up-
bringing. They might even have been able to explain the
visions and why I was different. If only they hadn't been
blown to...

Although this is a train of thought that has coursed
through the station of my mind countless times, this time, a
new bell is rung: is there some kind of connection between
the explosion and my abilities? Something my parents knew
about?

I think about the last time I talked about my parents with
Aunt Mayella; it was about a week before she died. She'd
been nervous, but that wasn't anything new, really. She said
that all the women in her family–including my mother, her
sister–were high strung. I had stopped asking Aunt Mayella
about my parents years ago when I had discovered a deep pit
of anger in myself directed toward them. I'd found that I was
really mad at them for leaving me behind. In a weird way, I'd
felt excluded. But as I got older, I'd felt the stirrings of curiosity again.

That day, a week before the car accident that killed her, I'd asked her about my father and his work. She'd told me before that it took him away for months at a time, but I questioned her more closely than I ever had before and brushed aside her vaguer explanations. She'd gotten more and more nervous but had finally told me that she would tell me more soon. In a few weeks. How about my birthday in December? I'd be seventeen then and ready to hear...well, everything, was how she put it.

I'd put a lot of it out of my mind with Aunt Mayella's death and my move to the hospital. I'd had a bit of a breakdown, it seems. I don't really remember it. But now I wonder if...

"Okay, we're up," True says, her voice tumbling down to me in shaky relief. "Hand me the lighter and I'll–"

She'd been reaching down to me and just as I was about to pass her the lighter, she screamed and was ripped from the ladder and into the darkness of the teepee above. I nearly dropped the lighter, but I managed to shove it in my pocket and then I scrambled up the remaining six feet of ladder.

Roger and the remaining Killen had True by the arms and were dragging her across the floor toward the opening. She kicked and thrashed in their grip trying to twist away. They were silhouetted and backlit by the afternoon sun as they dragged her outside.

I burst through the doorway only seconds behind them

and was instantly blinded by the light. I threw an arm over my eyes, shielding them. I didn't close them, because I wanted to acclimate as quickly as possible. In the crook of my elbow, orange and yellow dappled a hot pattern on my retinas.

"True! True, which way? Which way?"

"JD, here! I'm here! Follow my voice, JD, help! Help me, ple–"

Another sickening slap and then a thud and then True is screaming. The scream was all rage and pain pouring out, and I felt the hot day grow cold around me. My heart leapt again into my throat.

Roger must have stabbed her.

I was already following the sound of her voice around the teepee, the structure rough under my hand as I followed it around, chasing the sound of her voice. When she screamed, I forgot about shielding my eyes and just ran, full tilt toward the sound of her screams. My hand had gone unconsciously to the lighter in my pocket and I pulled it out. A large, struggling shadow was before me. It looked as though a tree had come to life and even blurry, I recognized it as the back of the Killen. I could just begin to make out True at its feet.

I struck the wheel of the lighter, still running, and launched myself at the Killen. Crashing into it was like crashing into a thicket, I felt small branches scratch my face and hands and arms where my skin was exposed.

My weight and the force of my charge tumbled us over

with me on top. The Killen had managed to turn itself as we crashed into the ground and it looked at me with its dead yet glittering onyx eyes. I recognized this one from the vision. This was that first rogue Killen. After all these years.

My hand was buried somewhere in its mid-section and when it burst into flames, I felt its arms tighten around me. It was going to force me to burn with it. The flames charged up its side, and I felt them simultaneously in my own side and also as the Killen…the small bond we'd made when…

…I'd seen it born and even as it looks at me I see myself through its eyes, my eyes round and afraid but determined, and it sees what I have that it doesn't have, what it can never be, it will never be human and suddenly it is tired, it is so tired, it's been too long existing as it has in the cold and howling half life of nothing and then its arms release me, layers of sand flow down over the onyx almost as though…

…it closes its eyes and its arms fall away and I roll off. Just in time, because it collapses in on itself as it burns and the flames jump up and release a burst of smoke that jumps even higher. I see True through the smoke; her eyes, too, are on the Killen as it burns. Her arm is canted at an odd angle in front of her and her eyes are glazed with pain. Her arm is broken; she hasn't been stabbed. Not yet.

Roger is kneeling above her, the knife raised over his head. His eyes are round with rage and loss as the Killen burns away. A low growl begins in the back of his throat and rises as he looks down at True, lying prone and dazed before him.

"Roger, no!" I shout, and he is distracted for a split second. I scramble up and over the Killen, kicking bits of its burning carcass back into the woods. I throw myself over True and she cries out in pain as I roll her away from the descending knife.

Roger lunges clumsily forward, never leaving his knees and the knife arcs down again. This time, it barely misses my leg and buries itself to the hilt in the sand. Roger's cry is one of frustrated rage, and his eyes on mine are black with fury.

True is in shock from her broken arm and I can't move her again, but I can't let Roger get to her. Keeping myself between her and Roger leaves me only one option: try and disarm him on the next strike.

Roger raises the knife again and I ready myself for it, trying to prepare to grasp the blade, even if it means slicing my hand open. It's my one shot. Roger's lips curl and every muscle in his body tightens in anticipation, when suddenly a high, despairing scream comes from behind him. It rings through the woods, inhuman and otherworldly and somehow innocent.

It's Pepper. The flames from the dying Killen have eaten trails through the dry woods and one of the trails, the largest one, has her cornered where True and I left her to keep her from harm.

A ten foot wall of flame is between us and her. She screams again, backing and kicking and trying to get herself away from the fire. Her sad panic rings in my head, but there is nothing I can do, I can't leave True to save Pepper.

But someone else can save her.

"Roger," I say, yelling to be heard over the deadly crackle of the fire and Pepper's screams. "That's Pepper! That's Pepper screaming! She's going to be burned alive if you don't do something! Please, Roger! Can't you hear her? She's your horse! Your responsibility!" I think I see a flicker of something, some recognition in his eyes. Doubt is replacing the rage. Awareness is replacing the distressing blankness. "Roger, she needs you! Pepper needs you to save her! Right now!"

Pepper screams again and awareness snaps fully into Roger's eyes. He blinks and looks dazedly at the knife in his hand. He is like someone coming awake.

"JD?" he says, looking from me to True and then back to the knife in his hand. Relief floods through me. Roger is back. "What happened? What did I–"

"Save Pepper! Roger, save her! She's going to burn if–" but I am talking to his back. Roger runs to Pepper and leaps straight through the flames. I can't see them, the fire is too dense, but I can make out a struggle.

The fire is so high now that the heat of it makes my eyes water. True is struggling up behind me and I reach for her shoulders to steady her. Her panicked eyes are on the fire. Tears wash clean tracks through the grit and soot on her face. "Pepper! Pepper is in there! That's where we left her!"

"Roger will save her!" The fire is so loud that we have to yell over it. In the short time since the Killen's end, it seems that half the woods have started burning.

"Roger?" she looks at me, uncomprehending. "But he tried to kill me! To kill us!"

I nod. "I know, but he's snapped out of it! With the last Killen gone and then with Pepper in trouble…I think he's himself again! I think it's–"

There's a roar behind me and I turn just in time to see Pepper come bursting through the curtain of flame. She seems to hang at the apex of her leap, muscular legs taut and gleaming. Her head is high and flames curl up and around her body like enormous, fiery wings. Her scream is one of triumph.

Roger is on her back.

The pines above us begin to sway in a hectic, fevered dance, pine needles falling in a light patter like green and tan snow. It seems almost as though Pepper's furious charge has brought the entire Pine Barrens to life around us.

Roger jumps from Pepper's back, and she stomps and shivers nervously, on the verge of bolting. The fire is still too close and getting closer. The flames are imprinted in her eyes. Roger runs a calming hand down her neck. He cups a hand around one of her twitching ears and puts his mouth to it, whispering, and Pepper calms.

Roger turns to me, yelling over the roaring fire. "We have to get True out of here! We can't all ride out on Pepper...can you run?"

I swallow and nod. I can run, yeah, but not as fast as the horse. I look past Roger at the fire, which is now consuming more than half of the area around us. This isn't looking good at all. Then I see an odd thing: a man is descending from the forest canopy. Silhouetted against the flames, he looks like a black angel. Then I see another. And another.

Everything snaps into place. There's a helicopter up there. That's why the trees were swaying. I couldn't hear it over the fire.

The black angels resolve into soldiers and the first one down is to us in seconds. "Are you JD?" he says, yelling over the roaring of the fire, and I feel another wave of surrealness wash over me. I nod. "Okay," the soldier says, "Dex sent us to come get you!" He nods toward True. "Is she okay?" True has lain back down and her face is very white where her tears have washed her skin clean.

"Her arm is broken; get her out first! How did Dex...?" The soldier shakes his head and turns away, yelling into a small box on his wrist. I can't make out what he is saying, but within seconds I see a stretcher being lowered.

The soldier stands as two others bundle True onto the

stretcher and ascend with her into the sky. I watch her go and another wave of unreality courses through me. It's all happening so fast. The first soldier turns to Roger.

"I'm taking JD next and then another soldier will take you up!" He puts a hand on Roger's shoulder. "I'm sorry, but we can't save the horse! We don't have the room or the time!"

Roger nods and steps back as the soldier straps me into a kind of papoose on his chest and then we're rising through the trees. The heat lessens as we rise and that's when I realize how hot it had gotten down there. I think about the dues ex machina I'd learned about in a in a high school English class and glance up at my own personal machina, blades patiently churning the black smoke. I am grateful beyond belief. I look back down for Roger and Pepper.

But they're gone.

-21-

This hospital is not like my hospital. The rooms are clean but stark. No comfortable reading chair here, in fact, the chair I'm sitting in is about as welcoming as...as a boulder. My first thought had been 'as welcoming as a pile of sticks' but I'm weeding any kind of stick reference from my mind. For the next little while, at least. Say, the next fifteen to twenty years.

"You should go home and change. You still smell like a fi–"

"Huh uh...don't say it." I put a finger gently over True's lips. "Not the 'f' word, not around me. And no 't' word, either."

She cocks her head on the pillow and smiles. "Okay, 'f' word I get, but 't'? What's the t-word?" Her voice is slightly raspy but mostly just tired. A white cast is on her arm. They insisted on keeping her overnight even though it's only late afternoon. I think Dex asked them to. He's got a lot of friends.

"Tree," I say, whispering it into her ear. I smile.

She laughs a little but it dies quickly. Concern clouds her features. "Roger?" she asks.

I shake my head. No Roger; not yet. No Pepper, either.

"It's only been a few hours," I say, but can hear the doubt in my own ears. The fire had taken off like...well...like wild fire. There are at least a hundred acres or more involved by now. They'd had to call in all the volunteers they could, because the local Ranger Station is down by four people–that's almost a third of the entire staff.

"Listen, I think that Roger will…will…"

"Be okay?"

I turn in surprise as Dex walks through the door. He's smiling and has me in a bear hug before I can even stand all the way up.

"Sorry I didn't get here sooner." He squeezes me once more. "We had to do a breaking report about the fire in the Barrens."

"Roger?" True says, struggling to sit up. I push the button, raising the bed for her. Her eyes don't leave Dex.

"He's out. He's fine…but…"

True had begun to smile but it faltered. I grab her hand.

"But?" I ask.

"He's been taken into custody by the State Troopers. Because of Stiles."

Stiles is in this hospital, too. I stopped in to see him while they were casting True's arm. He's stable but not coherent yet. I had wanted to stay longer, but the Troopers already in there made me nervous. They had a very 'closed ranks' attitude and it was obvious they were anxious for me to be gone. I can understand it. Stiles is a good officer, but more importantly, he's a good man…someone you want to have around.

For a long time.

"True, I want to apologize to you," Dex says, leaning forward and offering her his hand. She takes it, but her face is confused. "For calling you a 'kid' back at that cabin. You know I didn't mean it, right?"

True nods, looking a little dazed. Dex at full force charm is probably a little overwhelming to True. He seems to sense it and he sits back, releasing her hand. Then I ask him something I'd been wondering since we got out of the Barrens.

"Dex, how did you know where to find us the second time? I didn't have my phone with me."

Dex smiles and motions me to him. He dips his fingers into the collar of my shirt. "This little guy," he says, holding a small black disk in his hand. A red dot of light pulses in its center and there's something that looks almost like Velcro on the back of it. I shake my head.

"What is it?" I ask.

"I attached this to your collar at the cabin," he says. "It's from my friends at the base." He smiles again but this time his smile is shuttered. It says 'don't ask'.

So I don't.

***

True's apartment table is small. Really it should only have four people around it, but we've crammed it full with six chairs.

She stands back, looking at it critically. Good smells are wafting from the small kitchen behind her. She rubs absently at her arm. The cast came off yesterday and her arm looks white and shrunken.

"Are you sure you want to do this? You're not too tired?" I ask. I'm worried…too much of the time.

She looks at me and all the fret leaves her face as she smiles. "I'm fine, JD. This is normal, believe me. Everyone gets a little anxious before a party." She hugs me, and I feel a roller coaster lift and drop in my stomach followed by the most remarkable sense of peace. I feel this way every time her arms go around me. I get a brief flash of her hugging me from an earlier age; she's a toddler, maybe or…maybe a little older than a toddler, maybe five or even six…where did this feeling come from?

I pull back to look at her. She's still smiling. "Did you decide yet?"

True has asked me to come live with her. I shrug and feel my face color, knowing I'm being an idiot, but unable to help myself. "How about next month? Can we talk about it then?" I don't want to disappoint her, but I've lived in the hospital for a long time. The thought of leaving it and being 'out here' is just…well, it's daunting. The grocery shopping we've been doing together is bad enough.

I am so afraid of hurting her, but when I meet her gaze,

there is no hurt in her eyes. Just love. And patience.

"I'm not hurt," she says. "I understand."

It's weird how she seems to read my mind. What is that? Does love make you psychic or what? As I ponder, the doorbell rings.

Nora is the first to arrive.

Nora and True have gotten very close over the last three months. There's a mutual admiration between them, but something more, too. Maybe it has something to do with the fact that Nora doesn't have any children and True doesn't have any parents, or maybe that's too simple to explain their developing relationship. Whatever the case may be, I'm happy for them both.

Nora hugs me first and then she and True go to the kitchen. True's voice is a bit higher than normal and questioning and Nora's is calm as she explains something about the correct temperature for baking a chicken. They each seem to enjoy the mother daughter roles they are taking on.

The doorbell rings again and this time it's Dex. He brings a bottle of wine and gracious compliments for the tiny table and the cramped apartment but then says he won't be able to stay for dessert. He has to be to the station by seven. Charming and busy as always.

Dex has poured Nora a glass of wine and she's questioning him closely regarding the teepee and the cavern beneath it. I had told her everything, of course; not as a doctor but as a friend. Dex is shaking his head.

"They didn't find it. Nothing like it." He throws me a brief smile, but I feel something veiled in his glance, something he is keeping to himself. "The fire leveled everything for over two hundred acres. If there was some kind of...giant teepee out there, well, it's gone now."

"But the cavern below it? Surely that wouldn't be gone?" Nora's disbelief is a bit theatrical. She must sense the reluctance in Dex, too. She's not psychic, not like me, but she has been his friend for a long time. Sometimes that's enough.

When he answers, his tone is level. "If it's there, they didn't find it."

"If?" True is standing in the kitchen doorway with a glass of wine in her hand. Her head is high and I am struck again by how beautiful she is. How strong.

"I meant 'if it's *still* there'," he says and smiles. "The people from the base haven't been able to locate a cavern, that's all I'm saying. Not that it matters anymore, right? You guys are out and you're fine and everything is good." He raises his glass and True and Nora raise theirs, smiling. "To JD and True," he says. "Cheers!"

The doorbell rings again.

I open it to Stiles and Roger standing shoulder to shoulder. Roger looks pissed off. They are each carrying an apple pie from the little shop in the center of town.

"I told him to get anything *other* than an apple pie,"

Roger says, moving past me and handing True the pie. He
brushes her cheek with a kiss then shakes Nora's hand and
then Dex's. "How are you Nora? Dex? He said he'd get cookies." Roger throws himself into a chair without taking his coat
off. He no longer wears feathers, or for that matter, American
Indian swag of any kind. In a weird way, I kind of miss it.
Although odd, it gave Roger some kind of character–almost
a bravado–that he lacks now. He looks like any other mid-
dle-aged guy you'd see on the street. I hope after a while he
decides to re-adopt at least the crow's feather he used to wear.

"First of all," Stiles says, shedding his coat and shaking
hands all around. His tone is as mild and affable as ever, even
if he is still limping and the scars on his face are still pink. "I
never said I'd get cookies. Second of all, I thought you said
to *get* an apple pie…not get anything *but* an apple pie."

Roger crosses his arms over his chest. He has been a different person since the incident. Subdued, a bit cranky, a little sad…not his old self. Part of it, of course, is the death of
the twins, Andrew and Jackson. He'll be a long time getting
over that. But there's something more, some fundamental
change in him. He's gotten older, all at once.

Not that I would know; I have to take True's word for it.

Stiles puts a hand on Roger's shoulder. "Okay, how about
this…we'll call it even. You tried to kill me and I ruined your
pie. We're square now; deal?"

Roger's mouth had dropped open and now he closes it

with a snap. Emotions flow over his face from embarrassment to shock but finally he settles on a smile. It is small, a bit chagrined, but it's there. Stiles smiles back and squeezes Roger's shoulder again.

Dex had been holding in laughter behind his hand but now he has to let it go. He actually snorts and then looks slightly disgusted with himself but then Nora laughs, too. Suddenly, the four of them are laughing and Roger is slapping Stiles on the back.

I get why they're laughing, I really do.

I just don't think it's funny. Maybe someday I will, but not now; not yet.

True catches my eye and her expression is somber. Then she gives me a small smile and a nod. It's going to be okay, she is saying. Then she turns to Roger, putting a glass before him.

"How is Pepper?" she asks him. He looks at True, a warm smile erasing the past three months of grief.

"She's beautiful, as always. Happy and content."

"I'm gad to hear it. Want to ride this weekend? It'll be too cold if we wait much longer."

Roger nods. "Love to, my dear."

"Nora, you should come with us," True says and then she sends me the briefest glance along with a sly wink. I know what she's doing. Playing matchmaker.

Dex snorts, taking in Nora's tailored suit and sensible pumps. "Nora? On a horse? Ha!"

"You don't know everything about me, pal," Nora says. "Listen…"

She starts to tell him about a horse she used to ride as a kid and I follow True into the kitchen. I help her stack plates and cups onto the little serving counter. We work in companionable silence. Then she smiles and gives me another hug. Nice. I hug her back tight.

"Everything's going to be okay," she says in my ear. "Everything is going back to normal."

I think she's right. Normal. Nice and normal. I can live with that.

"JD," Nora says from the kitchen doorway. Dex and Roger are still at the table, laughing at something Stiles just said. "Sorry to interrupt, but can I talk to you for a second? In private? It's important."

There is a newspaper clipping in her hand.

Oh, no.

The End

***

Following is the beginning of:
Faith Creation, All Lies Revealed
Book One in the Faith Series

Christine Dougherty

PROLOGUE: 1978

The first time my sister died, we were three years old.

I was sitting up, my back to the cold cinderblock wall, looking across to her bed. I had pulled my blanket to my chest and gripped a worn stuffed animal under my chin. The room was gray and dim; the only light the one that hung over her like a spotlight. Adults surrounded her. They were tall and faceless behind masks, featureless even down to their identical, black, elbow-length gloves. I caught glimpses of my sister between their shadowed forms. Her small face was still and pale, framed by feathery black hair.

Her face was my face.

Her lips had gone from pink to an unnatural, bluish white; they looked very cold. I checked the dark, secret spot in my mind (…ellie?…), questing for any small hint of life but found none, only cold emptiness where she'd always been before.

I touched my own lips to see if they were warm. Or cold.

The adults murmured above her, their conversation quiet snatches beyond my comprehension.

"Told them before that…"

"At this rate, we won't have enough to…"

"…too delicate for this…"

"…just too unstable, that's all, and…"

"Okay, let's bag her. The lab is going to need…"

Did they see me sitting up in the next bed over? I don't remember receiving any measure of comfort or reassurance as tears rolled from my eyes and burned across my cheeks.

She was zipped into a yellow, plastic bag that turned her into a small, anonymous bundle. An attendant carried her from the room. He carried her casually, under one arm, as you'd hoist any ordinary burden. Two others stayed behind to strip the bed. They still wore masks over their faces and gloves on their hands.

When they finished, they left, clicking off the overhead light. I don't recall any other type of light in the room—nightlight, star shine, or moonshine. Only blackness.

I curled onto my side and pulled the blanket over my shoulder, my animal clutched to my chest. It was a rabbit, made of soft and hard patches; fur and the places where my nervous hands had rubbed the fur away.

"...ellie..." I thought, crying and miserably afraid.

CHAPTER ONE: 1997

"Are you going to stay in this house?"

Lotte is back from wherever it was she took Grandfather. I had asked if I could go with her, help see to his new surroundings, but she said it was better that I didn't. I had wanted to protest, but in the end of course, I didn't. Even at twenty-two, I am still accustomed to following Lotte's directives. Hers has been the voice of rule since she moved in eleven years ago to help Grandfather through his illness.

I am on the sofa, reading, when she asks if I am going to stay in the house. She stands in the living room doorway, her back to the kitchen. I lower my book and look around to her, keeping my face neutral to hide my confusion. It's never good to give Lotte too much insight to anything I'm feeling. I consider the hard wooden chairs, gray-green rug, cold fireplace and drab walls. Am I going to stay? Where else would I go? This is the only place I've ever lived. The only place I can remember, anyway.

I look at her and shrug. "I hadn't thought about it."

"You'll have to think about it now, Faith." she says, turning back into the kitchen.

Lotte is wide, but solid, not fat. She looks as though if you thumped her, you'd hear the dense, gelatinous tone of a barrel filled with sludge. Not that I would think of thumping

Lotte. Her hair is the same close-cropped, gray cap that it has been for as long as I've known her. I know she is younger than Grandfather, but it's hard to say by how much.

I don't like Lotte but I don't dislike her, either. Lotte is like a fact of nature, an intractable truth. She doesn't explain, she proclaims, yet seems to have no interest in whether you care for, or even heed, her proclamations. She is like an impassive blackjack dealer, laying out the cards, indifferent to either your sudden good fortune or disastrous ruination.

The thought of leaving this house scares me. I don't have anything or anywhere else. I have stayed here, a recluse, a freak. A Boo Radley bereft of shy charm or woodworking skills. Were any child to happen upon me, I am sure they would run, screaming, from the obviousness of my fundamentally inhuman nature.

I confess none of this to Lotte. As far as I am aware, she's never had one second's worth of self-doubt. She has no frame of reference for human failings. I had tried, once, to discuss with her the memory of my sister dying and the way it has stayed with me, coloring everything in my life. Making me feel wary and unsure. She had turned away, unimpressed and unmoved.

I worry over the memory of my sister dying incessantly and have never been able to make it an un-memory, *not* remembered as Lotte–and before her, my grandmother–would seem to want it to become.

Grandmother had told me that it was a dream induced by fever. I didn't then and still don't believe her. Her explanation seemed thin, especially in light of things that occurred later on. Plus, Charity and I had never been sick. Never a day in our lives.

She had tried to tell me how I woke, screaming for Charity, burning in the night. After repeated questioning, she had finally put her foot down and refused to discuss it any further. Like Lotte, Grandmother'd had no patience for frailty of feeling, either.

I lay down my book and go to the front window. This neighborhood has large homes, each sitting on at least two acres of ground with a line of woods between each. The view is well known to me because I stare out this window more than I watch television in the back den. But today, I barely see the yard. I turn the old memory over and over in my mind, trying to see under and around it. There is something familiar, something that I miss; no matter how much I examine it.

When we were younger, I had brought it up often to Charity. Depending on her mood, she would listen to the story of her demise with rapture, amusement, or annoyance.

"I didn't *die*, Faith," Charity had said, not looking up from the book open beside her plate.

I had shrugged and turned away from the light impatience in her voice. We'd been in the grandparent's kitchen, on the morning of the first day of fifth grade. The kitchen was large and beige and white. The only flashes of color were unintentional, unavoidable—a dash of blue on the egg carton, the red tomato juice in our glasses, the green leaves basted with early autumn sunshine. The handful of pale pink, white, and salmon vitamins beside our plates.

We only ever ate breakfast in the kitchen. Dinner was eaten in the dining room. Lunch was eaten at school or in our room.

I remember turning my face to the light coming through the window, leaning my head on my hand and closing my eyes. The sun was warm and bloomed yellow and orange patterns on my eyelids. Without opening my eyes, I had said, "It wasn't a dream, Charity."

She'd heaved an audible sigh and closed the book. "Here I *am*, though," she'd said, "sitting right next to you." She'd bumped my shoulder with hers.

I had smiled, opened my eyes and turned to face her. The sun left an after-image on my retinas, and Charity had seemed to be surrounded by a warm, yellow corona. Her black hair looked soft and feathery and shined prettily, the sun picking out red highlights that seemed to glow with a light of their own. Her eyes were sparkling emeralds.

"Yes, here you are," I'd said and bumped her back.

Grandmother had been at the stove making eggs, her back to us as usual. Back in those days, we would eat eggs three times a week, oatmeal twice, and cereal twice. This had never varied, no matter the season. Grandmother had been wearing a white blouse and black skirt. This also had never varied season to season. They weren't always the same blouse and skirt, but they were so plain, they might as well have been.

She had paid no attention to our conversation; she never did. Only if we laughed too loud would she comment, telling us to control ourselves. If we cried, she would leave us to our own devices, and you could tell she didn't like the crying, either. We'd gotten very good at managing ourselves. By age ten, we would rarely cry or laugh if either of the grandparents were nearby.

On that September morning, Grandfather had been out back coaxing the last of the summer vegetables from his garden—we could hear him through the screen door. He had always talked to his plants. His indulgent, admiring tone had been foreign to Charity and me. Maybe he liked the plants better because he got something usable from them. We'd never been as engaging as the tomato plants and cucumbers, and he got nothing from us but occasional vials of blood and forced coughs for his cold stethoscope.

Charity and I had always kept to ourselves. We were content to have each other because we were identical twins. We were a closed unit.

The grandparents had taken us in when we were very little, after our mother died in an apartment fire. Charity and I had no recollection of her or of anything before coming here.

Grandmother had said we were fairly sickly, implying that our mother hadn't been a very good one. Implying, too, that we were even more of an inconvenience than Grandmother could have anticipated; certainly more of a burden than she wanted or deserved. The grandparents took us in because, according to them, there was no one else. But I think they were too old to raise us. The living arrangement seemed as uncomfortable for them as it was for Charity and me. Only Grandmother had been involved in the details of our daily routines, eating, dressing, school…while Grandfather'd only been in charge of our overall state of health. I wouldn't say well-being.

We used take turns being our own mom. I would lie in bed with the covers pulled to my chin, and Charity would read a story from the handful of books we had found stored haphazardly in a far corner of the basement. She would brush the hair from my forehead and say, "Now you must go to sleep, darling, but mommy will stay right here until you do." And her voice would be honeyed and calm.

Other times, I would be the mommy and put my wrist to Charity's forehead and shake my head. "Darling," I would say, "you've got a fever…we'll have to get you to the doctor first thing in the morning. I'm afraid I'll have to keep you home from school for a few days."

We had known that mothers did these things; we'd overheard it at school as kids discussed it around us. We understood that the mothers took your temperature and fussed over you and took you to the doctor. The doctor was for shots or for a sore throat or for spraining something—a wrist or an ankle.

But Charity and I had never been to the doctor. In our memory, we'd never been sick.

Grandfather was the one who took our temperatures, measured our height and weight, and took blood from our fingers or (twice a year) a tube full from our arms. One time, Charity had asked Grandmother if Grandfather was a doctor. Grandmother's face had gone even paler than usual, and a tight knot had appeared at her jaw line. She'd turned and hurried from the room, banging her hip on the table on the way, making our breakfast dishes jump and clatter.

It was always tricky, asking Grandmother something, and we had to be careful. You were never sure how she was going to react.

We were born on April 1, 1975. Grandmother had told us that our mother had been their only child. She had claimed to have no idea who our father was. The only kind thing she ever said about our mother was that she had been beautiful; and that Charity and I had gotten our black hair and green eyes from her.

There was one picture of my grandparents that hung in the front hall–Grandmother and Grandfather on their wedding day. They were old even in their wedding picture.

Grandfather's straight across smile and Grandmother's tight-lipped, shallow curve were more or less their everyday expressions. The only indication of the occasion was the bouquet of tiny pink roses Grandmother held next to her leg like an afterthought. They didn't touch each other. There was no one else in the picture.

We'd had one picture of our mother. In it, she is in a hospital, a baby in her arms. Her black hair is swept casually back from her forehead as if she'd just run her hands through it. Her eyes are dark green, and she is smiling. But it must have been almost immediately after our births, because there is also a deep shadow of pain in her eyes. A trick of the light or the angle of the picture gives her an expression that is almost distrustful. She is looking at someone standing behind and to the right of whoever is taking the picture. The date burned into the corner reads 04/01/75 8:32 AM.

I say it is Charity in the picture, and she says it is me. Secretly, I hope it *is* me, just as she hopes it is her. We each spend a lot of time staring at it, but we do it separately. It was easier to settle into fantasies of being the baby in this woman's arms when you didn't have your sister's mind nattering away beside you with fantasies of her own. The edges of the picture were frayed and we had approached Grandmother about getting a copy made—two copies, so Charity and I could each have one. We had asked this for a Christmas present. But we never got them.

We had scoured the grandparent's house, looking for other pictures. It was the one thing we did on a consistent basis that we thought could potentially bring punishment. So, we did it in secret.

Charity and I would take turns searching. One of us would engage Grandmother in conversation while the other quietly rummaged in drawers and on shadowed shelves. You had to be quick, though, because Grandmother never let herself be held long. There wasn't much to talk to her about. We had little to offer that would hold her attention.

We craved evidence of our mother's own babyhood, girlhood and teenage years. We'd gone through drawers and kitchen cupboards, the pantry and our grandparent's closet. We'd been through the basement and into the attic without turning up any indication of our mother's existence. Had they, in their sorrow over her death, simply gotten rid of all evidence of her? Was that something grieving parents did?

There were no other pictures of the grandparents, either. Nor were there any of us.

We did find files dedicated–in a way–to our growing up. There were in two black metal cabinets in Grandfather's study, side by side, under the windows. The files began on September 1st, 1976 and continued on from there. The notations are, at first, weekly accounts of our weight, height, diet, words we said…kind of a charting of our progress. When we'd started kindergarten, the notations had become monthly.

Interspersed with the handwritten notes were pictures—not photographs, but finger paintings and crayon drawings. We knew we must have done these in school because we have no crayons, paints or colored pencils of any kind here. We've never had anything like that in this house.

I would take them out, carefully noting the file they had come from, and try and decide what about these particular pictures made them worthy of being kept. Our grandparents had never put drawings on the refrigerator or allowed us to tape our creations to our bedroom walls. This was a home untouched by vibrancy of any kind, and any artistic activity, as far as the grandparents seemed concerned, was to be done only at school.

I never had been able to figure out why those pictures were the ones that had been saved. In the grandparent's house, it was easier to understand what you had done wrong than to see what you had done right.

CHAPTER TWO

"You're going to have to give it some thought, now, because I'm not going to be here. I'm moving back to Trenton," Lotte says and spares me a glance as she sips her coffee. Her eyes are pale gray. Then she looks speculatively around the living room. "You'll have to decide if you're going to stay or go."

"But...sell this house you mean?" I ask. "I wouldn't know how. Although, I guess I could use the money to..."

Lotte shakes her head, looking past me and out the window. Spring is almost here. The last of the snow peeks out from the ditches where it huddles in dirty shame, having been pushed there days ago by the plows.

"You can't sell it; it isn't yours."

"Well, when...if, I mean, if Grandfather dies. Then it will be mine."

"I'm afraid it isn't his, either," she says. "Your grandparents didn't own this house."

"They were renters?"

"Not exactly, no."

I shake my head. One quick, small shake. I am starting to feel exasperated. "Well, but what then? If they don't own it and aren't renters, what else is there?"

Lotte stares at me, levelly, for a full minute. Then she

takes another sip of coffee. "I'm afraid that isn't for me to say. It was their business."

"I don't understand. You made it sound as though staying was an option. For how long? Until Grandfather dies?"

"No, you can stay as long as you like."

I cross my arms over my chest, confused, but trying to keep the distress from my voice. "I can stay here indefinitely, but I can't sell it," I say. "Do I have to pay some sort of…rent or fee or something?"

Lotte shakes her head. "No."

"Who owns this house?" I ask.

"I can't tell you that."

"Can't because you don't know or won't because…"

"It's not my business, it's your grandfather's. It's not my place. You should talk to him about it."

I picture my drooling, staring, cataleptic grandfather and bark out a short, unfunny laugh. "You could have told me that three years ago," I say.

Lotte shrugs, unperturbed. "You could have asked."

And of course, she is right.

I have spent the last twelve years of my life with my head in a book, my mind on nothing, concentrating only on *not* seeing, *not* reaching out, trying to give no thought to my physical world. Beyond eating, sleeping, reading…there has been almost nothing else. One day bleeding into another, I have been like a sleepwalker, but now it is as though Lotte has tilted everything out of alignment; shaken me from my long sleepwalk by pulling not just the rug, but the floor–the entire house–out from under me. I don't want to live here with Lotte, but I don't want to live here without her, either. Where would the food come from? The clothes? How would I *get* anything?

That night in my room, I look in the full-length mirror on the closet door. I see my bed reflected, and I shift my gaze until Charity's bed is in there with mine–our twin beds. I see our dresser, our desk and window; there isn't much else to see in our sad, plain little room and finally, reluctantly, I look at myself, standing in my nightgown and robe.

I am tall. At thirteen, I had started to grow and by fifteen, had been almost as tall as Grandfather. The last time he measured me, he said I was five feet and ten inches; that had been when I was sixteen. My black hair hangs to the small of my back. I usually wear it in a braid to keep it off my face and out of my way. My skin is pale, untouched by sun. I shift my robe back over my shoulders and shrug it onto the ground.

I look at my arms in the mirror. The warm light from the bedside lamp is kind and softens the solid lines of the muscles that curve under my skin. The curves are gentle undulations, but the muscles themselves are hard as rock, as iron. I make two fists and watch my forearms contract, the tendons at my elbows standing out, throwing sharp shadows back onto my biceps. Even Grandfather's arms, strong and sinewy as they were, didn't compare to mine. My anatomy is freak-ish, even in soft light.

Finally, I look at my face. My lips are pink, and there is a pink flush in my cheeks. My eyes are dark in the dim room, clouded and murky. My eyebrows are black like my hair, and they are straight across, level and without a curve. I can see her. Just below the lines of my face is the softer, rounder face we shared in childhood. *Charity*, I think, *I see you...I miss you*. She smiles, but as she does, my twenty-two year old face reasserts itself. I am left without her. Again.

I am filled with a sense of longing so deep that it becomes a physical ache, compressing my heart, slowing it, as my stomach rolls over on itself. My throat closes, and I swallow, trying to clear it, but it is painful. I climb under my covers and stare across to Charity's empty bed. The taupe blanket and pale sheets are made up, pulled tightly into place. Her rabbit rests on the pillow, staring forlornly at the ceiling. My own rabbit is long gone. Loved to death. Worried to death.

I want to see Charity so badly. I want to see the other half of me, my real life mirror image.

I remember that right before we'd started kindergarten, I had overheard Grandmother saying that our being twins was our curse. She hadn't said twins, she'd said that being the *same* was our curse, but of course, she'd meant being twins.

Maybe there *was* some curse to Charity and I, but what we'd felt with each other was pure comfort. I could always find her, even when we weren't in a room together. It's not that we always talked to each other without speaking–not like mind reading, although we did that, too–mostly it was more of a pulse, a warm spot, as though a small portion of Charity resided in my mind, and when I checked on her, I was simultaneously checking on the real, living Charity in the world. And of course, looking at Charity was the same as looking at myself.

We hadn't known that being twins might be something someone would find exciting. But I remember that, when we'd started kindergarten, the teacher had exclaimed over Charity and I, excited by our identical faces.

"If I had the two of you, I'd put you in matching outfits!" Miss Reddy had told us when we came to her classroom on our first day. She had been young and sweet faced; a little giddy. Charity and I had never seen anyone so animated, so engaging. The excess emotion pouring from Miss Reddy had made us uneasy.

"Faith, you'll sit here, and of course, I'll put Charity right next to you. Faith and Charity, my goodness!" she'd said, directing us to the little desks. "Your mommy must have been a bible reader!"

Charity and I had looked at each other, our interest piqued by mention of our mother, but bewildered by the rest of Miss Reddy's words.

"Did you know our mother?" I had asked.

Miss Reddy had blinked at me, her pink, shimmery lips forming a silent oh! of surprise.

"What's a bible?" Charity had asked her, when it seemed Miss Reddy wasn't going to answer my question.

She'd turned to Charity with a sharp intake of breath. The other children had swirled around us, chattering and excited. Miss Reddy was pulled from her confusion by a wail from the front of the classroom. A little blonde had stumbled over a boy who had bent to adjust the sock in his shoe. Miss Reddy had flown up the aisle, singing out, "Oh, honey, did oo take a widdle tumble?"

Charity and I had stared after her, wide eyed with astonishment. If we'd ever heard baby talk, it would have been during a time before we could recall.

Later that morning, when the other children napped, Miss Reddy had led Charity and me into the hall. She squatted down in front of us, smiling. She'd been fingering the small man on her necklace. The man was flying; arms spread wide, head down against the force of the wind.

"Don't you girls know what a Bible is?"

Charity and I had glanced at each other and then shaken our heads. I sensed a growing distress in Charity. She'd always been better than me at seeing a bad situation coming. But I wasn't distressed...I'd been too intrigued by Miss Reddy's comment about our mother.

"Your names are from the Bible. The Bible is a great book

that teaches us about God and how he created the whole world for us to live in. He created the mountains and the oceans and all the animals. And then he created us. Do you know who God is?"

I thought for a minute. I'd only known one person who seemed authoritative enough and capable enough to create things. "Is it Grandfather?"

"No, dear," she'd said and grasped our hands. "God is the Father of all mankind."

She had smiled again, a smile lit with breathless joy as if she had just told us that today was her birthday, and she knew there was a surprise party planned.

"Is he our father, too? Did you know him?" I had asked, getting excited. Maybe she had a picture she could show us. "Did you know our mother?"

Miss Reddy had started to look distressed. She'd reached out and grasped my shoulders. "Faith, do you know who Jesus is?"

I was getting impatient. Did she know our parents or not? "Is Jesus our father?"

"Yes, that's right! He is! You see..." Her eyes were bright, but a little desperate, almost feverish. I'd felt an answering flash of heat from Charity, and suddenly, Charity was crying, hiding behind her hands as tears coursed down her cheeks.

"Oh dear..." Miss Reddy had said, "Oh my gosh..."

I had glanced at Charity but then refocused my attention on Miss Reddy, galvanized. She was talking about our father! I'd never felt so close to getting an answer of some kind. "Grandmother says she doesn't know who our father was...do you have a picture of him? Can we see it? Can we meet him?"

Dawning realization had clouded Miss Reddy's sunny face as she'd fumbled for words. "Faith...I...what I meant was...I'm so sorry...I didn't mean, like, your real dad, I meant, like..."

The last vestiges of adult authority had puddled at Miss Reddy's feet as she backed away from our distress, hands fluttering near her neck.

Charity's sobbing had seeped fully into my mind, a purple pulse of misery, and then I was crying, too, overwhelmed by the nearness of something snatched brutally away. We had turned and clung to each other. I was so disappointed.

Miss Reddy had called the school nurse who had taken us down to her closet-like area near the front office. There was a desk, two chairs and a cot screened by a hanging curtain. She'd gotten us each a paper cup of water and then sat with us until we'd calmed. I had tried to tell her about our father and Jesus, and her lips tightened. She had disappeared and then we were talking to a lady in a suit jacket and skirt who told us she was the principal. She had explained that she was in charge of the school and responsible for all the students–

and teachers–in it. She looked as old as Grandmother, but not as severe. She'd led us from the nurse's office to hers and then called Grandmother.

When Grandmother had arrived, Charity and I had sat in the hall as the principal and Grandmother talked. I had been able to see them through the glass in the door. When she had been talking to us, the principal's face had been calm and open…friendly. Now, it was pinched and pale.

Grandmother hadn't shouted; she'd used her sly and slippery snake's voice on the principal. We caught only a bit of the exchange.

"…thought this was a public school, if I wanted them schooled with a bunch of religious nonsense…" from Grandmother.

"I'm sure that Miss Reddy meant no harm, she's a first year teacher, and…" from the principal.

"…certainly wouldn't want everyone knowing our personal…"

"Of course not! At this school we pride ourselves on…"

"I'm afraid she'll have to go…terrible influence on young minds…"

"…we didn't even have it in our records that their mother had died. Why haven't you notified…"

"It's our business, and…"

"…but if Miss Reddy had known, she wouldn't have…"

"Enough," Grandmother had said firmly, putting one

hand up, palm to the principal. Then she stood and leaned over the desk, and I saw the principal's mouth drop open. Grandmother had talked for another minute, but so quietly, we hadn't even been able catch her tone. Then she'd stood straight, adjusted her coat and tilted her head inquiringly to the principal. The principal had nodded her head, dropping her eyes. Then she'd glanced out the door at us. Her face was full of a pity and compassion I didn't understand.

The next day, there had been another lady teaching the class. She was older than Miss Reddy and much less animated. She didn't have much to do with Charity and I. She hadn't been unkind, just…distant. She had seemed wary and cautious, glancing at us and quickly away.

All the teachers had been that way ever since.

CHAPTER THREE

"I heard you crying last night," Lotte says at breakfast the next morning. "That makes eight nights in a row this time."

I don't say anything, just drink my coffee and look at the tabletop. I can feel my cheeks getting pinker. I'm glad I haven't braided my hair yet today as it falls like a veil over my face, hiding my shame.

"Charity?" she asks. I can hear her raised eyebrows.

I nod.

She sighs and sits back in her chair. "Faith, it's been twelve years."

I nod, again.

Lotte heaves a long, burdened sigh. "I'll have to find you something to do." She says this quietly, almost to herself.

I look up as a cramp of nervousness tightens my stomach. "What do you mean?"

"I mean you're a perfectly able bodied young woman. I know you haven't spent much time…out in the world." She lowers her head and purses her lips. I watch, fascinated. Is it chagrin on her face? Guilt? Something else?

"I know that it's at least in part my fault," she continues. The halting flow of her words shows these sentences—these very ideas—are difficult for her to contemplate, much less express. "I never thought, or that is, we never thought…"

"We?" I ask.

"Your grandfather and I," she says, but her eyes shift from mine when she says it. For the first time since I can remember, Lotte has told me an obvious lie.

The idea of looking into Lotte's mind appears and then is gone so quickly I am barely aware that I thought it. Nausea and unease follow and I have a brief flash of a teacher, on her knees, staring up at me, and I am seeing myself through her eyes…inhuman, monstrous. I feel a bubble of something in my stomach and my chest, some sort of information that I desperately don't want to acknowledge. I push it back down, unexamined. I train my thoughts back to what Lotte is saying.

"Maybe I could help you find a job," Lotte says. "It will get you out of this house. It might help with everything else, too." She means the crying.

"A job?" I shake my head. "I can't do anything."

"You might be surprised," Lotte says, raising her eyebrows but looking into her coffee cup. Again, it is almost as if she is talking to herself.

"What do you mean?"

She shifts in her chair and looks back up at me. "I think I can find you something to do," she says, standing. "That's all I meant."

I'd never considered a job…I'd never *done* anything. But I knew I was smart. Maybe that was what Lotte meant when she said I'd be surprised.

From kindergarten, Charity and I knew that we were more advanced than the other kids. We'd been reading for as far back as we could remember. The grandparents neither encouraged nor restricted this practice. We had quickly outgrown our handful of baby books and then only had the grandparent's library to choose from.

Grandfather's books were incomprehensible. We had looked through them because the pictures were interesting, but most of the text was beyond our understanding. They were medical books, with illustrations of the inner workings of every part of the human body. I was especially fascinated by a black and white line drawing of a hand, skin peeled back, muscles labeled, nerves and veins sharply delineated. I would look at my own soft hand, flex my fingers and marvel that so much went on under the skin. If I'd concentrated hard enough, I had been able to feel the individual muscles and tendons working and pulling, and then I'd begin to hear the tiny whoosh whoosh of blood through my veins. I could feel the blood moving, a certain hot and coldness, almost a tickle, as it pumped through my body. Sometimes it even made me a little dizzy, but that was only if I was concentrating too hard.

Grandmother's books had been more accessible, but just barely. Moby Dick, Little Women, The Call of The Wild, The Good Wife, The Secret Garden, Wuthering Heights…it was these books that had given us a different way to view the world. Especially once we'd started in school, it became clear just how odd our lives were.

I never blamed the other kids in our class for their aversion to Charity and I. The older I got and the greater my realization of our abnormal circumstances, the more I understood why we were considered strange. By the time we were in fifth grade, Charity and I had no interaction with our classmates even as the teachers had continued to quietly shun us.

When Evelyn Ames had joined our fifth grade class in the fall of 1985, she brought a change, and it was a change that didn't bode well for Charity and I. Evelyn was a big girl with white blond hair that hung in an even pageboy to her shoulders. Not typical of transfer students, she'd acted boisterous and outgoing. And she had disliked us at first sight.

"Who are the freaks?" she'd asked Mimi Jacob, the girl next to her. I had sat two seats behind Evelyn and Charity was two seats behind Mimi. The teacher had been standing in the hall waiting for stragglers, and the kids who heard Evelyn's question looked at Charity and me. Anyone who didn't hear was alerted by their classmates, and they had turned to pay attention, too. Excitement had rippled from desk to desk. Everyone knew who "the freaks" were.

Mimi had giggled, her hands covering her mouth, eyes wide with scandal. "That's Charity and Faith," she'd leaned closer to Evelyn and whispered loudly, loudly enough for us to hear. "They don't have parents."

Evelyn's eyebrows rose, and she'd looked back at us with great interest. "Hey Freak," she'd said, looking at me, "where's your parents? Or were you two hatched from an egg?"

A gusty sigh had traveled through the class as kids gasped or laughed. Charity and I were like a long held secret–something shameful and slightly nasty and better left undiscussed. But now Evelyn had come and shone a light on us.

Charity had looked at me, and a small pulse of unease coursed through my mind along with a question, unformed, but no less understandable (...why is she?...) and for which I had no answer. I had tossed Charity a reassuring thread but kept my attention focused on the big blonde girl.

"Our mom is dead." I'd said.

Mimi's eyes had gone round, and her mouth dropped open. She was looking at me, directly at me, for the first time since I could remember. "I didn't know that..." she'd started.

Evelyn, seeming to sense the other girls might warm to us said, "So? What about your dad, then? Is he dead, too?" Her callousness had caused a deep stirring in my stomach–a low, burning sensation had started to warm my insides.

"We don't have a dad."

In the world of children, a dead mother was sad and pitiable. No one could imagine a life without their mother. But to not have a dad, either? That was neither sad nor pitiable—it was just weird.

"What do you mean?' Evelyn had asked, "Did they get divorced? Is that what killed your mom?" Her chin had gone up as her eyes slitted halfway closed. No matter the answer, I knew she'd deem it the wrong one. Her casually cruel reference to our dead mother scared the other kids. You could see in their frightened and disbelieving eyes a realization that anyone who held a dead mother so lightly was probably a dangerous person; someone you wanted to stay on the good side of.

I had tried to skirt the question, not wanting to give her more reason to ridicule us. "We live with our grandparents."

"Oh, gross!" Evelyn had said, her blue eyes going round in mock shock and disgust. "I guess that's why you two smell like old lady underwear!"

A collective gasp from the class had preceded their laughter. The joke hadn't been that funny, and the laughter had sounded forced; it was the attack in itself that had been so provoking.

Evelyn had turned and casually faced front, dismissing me. Mimi and the three other girls nearest to her had all leaned in and started to ask Evelyn where she had gone to school before this one, why had her parents moved here, where was her house?

Charity's misery had eased, but my own anger had continued to burn. I had stared at the back of Evelyn's blond, swaying pageboy as she nodded to first one girl and then another, a queen acknowledging her court. I reached out in building resentment to Evelyn's mind…and I found her.

Whenever I checked on Charity, I didn't need to reach *out* to her, I simply looked into my own mind at the Charity that existed there. Reaching *into* Evelyn's mind had been a revelation.

The little (evelyn) inside the big Evelyn had been cowering in the black depths, desperately unhappy. She'd been terrified of doing or saying the wrong thing. She hadn't been well liked in her last school and had been the butt of jokes because of her height. Her first, desperate course of action at this new school had been to go on the offensive. Charity and I had seemed easy targets.

As the teacher had entered and the class finally quieted, Evelyn had turned and glanced back at me. Everything I had intuited was evident in her nervous eyes and raised eyebrows. I lowered my head slightly in acknowledgment and tried something else I'd never tried before…I had sent out a small tendril (…you better leave us alone…). Evelyn had jumped and faced forward but sent one more glance back my way. There had been real fear in her eyes. I could sense the little (evelyn) curling in on herself, turning away and hiding from me.

After my first flush of righteous excitement, the exchange had left me confused and ashamed. It hadn't seemed right, what I had done to Evelyn. It was like peeking at someone through a keyhole. Peeking at them in the bathroom, even. But it was even worse than that, because when you peeked at someone, you only *saw* them. But when I *reached*, I understood things about her that she didn't even seem to understand herself.

I *knew* her.

For a time after that first confrontation, Evelyn had steered clear of us, but as the weeks passed, she seemed to convince herself that those scared feelings could be attributed to first day jitters, and she had begun a sly, steady campaign against us. Before Evelyn, we had existed in anonymity. Our classmates talked neither to nor about us. The teachers' aloofness each year, their hands-off approach to my sister and me, had trickled through the ranks until it became accepted as standard behavior.

As a younger child, I had been content with this; it seemed safer to be separate from the other kids; from people in general. But eventually, I began to question the assumption that Charity and I should remain so secluded.

When we were in our first years of school, we had watched the other kids' moms with curiosity and envy, but as I got older, I found myself watching the kids themselves with the same feelings of envy and longing. I had wanted to try and be part of their games, conversations, jokes…I wanted that sense of *belonging*. I loved Charity, but our group of two had begun to seem woefully small. Especially as I had begun to realize that the grandparents couldn't really be counted as allies.

The boys and girls–especially the girls–had friendships of a casual intimacy that I desired. When Charity and I had readied ourselves for fifth grade, my main thought had been to try and begin to make inroads with the kids around us. At ten, I had felt that I finally knew enough and *understood* enough to be able to begin a tentative move toward making friends. But Evelyn showing up had put an end to my plans before I'd had much of a chance to begin.

By early October, she had completely forgotten her fear and had gotten bolder with her taunts. "Free-eeks," she had said one day, singing it when we'd passed by her table in the lunchroom. She'd sat with five other girls, and they had all laughed. Some covered their mouths, pretending shock, but their eyes slid over us cruelly. Their stares had made me feel like an animal whose den had been kicked apart.

Charity and I had sat with our lunch trays–macaroni and cheese and milk. We ate lunch at school every day, no matter what they served. No bright and cheerful lunchboxes for us. Grandmother gave us the tickets that qualified you for the school lunch; she gave us an entire years worth at the beginning of each grade. We had learned quickly not to lose the tickets.

On this day, waves of despair had flowed from Charity.

You didn't have to be her twin to see it. Her head had gone down, black hair feathered over her eyes, obscuring them from view. She had pushed her macaroni and cheese back and forth but didn't raise the fork to her mouth. The lunchroom, which was also the gymnasium, had twenty tables that the janitor rolled out for lunch and then collapsed and rolled away in time for gym later in the day. Each table could hold ten kids. Our table held two.

"Don't you want your macaroni?" I had asked.

Charity had shaken her head without raising it.

"Charity, what is it?"

"It's *her*, that Evelyn," she'd said. "She made everyone hate us." Then she'd raised her head, brushing her hair behind her ears. Tears shimmered at her lower lids.

"Take a drink of milk. Don't cry." Charity cried easily, and I didn't want Evelyn to know she was getting to us. I didn't see any chance anymore to make friends with the other kids, so the best I could hope for was a return to our original cover.

Charity had lifted her carton and took a tentative sip. She had swallowed hard, as if there were something more than milk she was trying to get down. Her lips had quivered and tightened, quivered and tightened as she tried to control her emotions.

"Free-eeks," had come drifting from behind me, and then again, louder…

"Oh, Free-eeeeks…"

Charity's tears had finally overrun her lids and slid in shiny trails down her cheeks. There was a burst of giggles from Evelyn's table. I had leaned over and put my hand on Charity's arm. "Charity, don't cry," I'd said. "That will make it worse." I had been starting to feel frantic: protective of Charity, angry at Evelyn, angry at the other girls…I had just wanted things to go back to the way they were before Evelyn got here.

There had been a shuffle at Evelyn's table as bodies parted to let someone stand up. I had looked around for Mrs. Hamm, the lunch monitor, but she must have stepped outside to smoke.

An arm had appeared between us and slammed a half eaten apple into Charity's macaroni and cheese. Charity had jumped as macaroni flew from the tray and landed in a splat on her shirt and skirt…there was even a smudge of runny, yellow cheese on her cheek. Her hands had flown to her face as she tried to cover her eyes. I had turned and Evelyn was standing next to me, hands on her hips. When she saw she had my attention, she gave me the finger. Everyone gasped. I had started to stand, but my knees were under the table, and I would have had to twist away from Evelyn to get my legs out. She had shoved me roughly back to the bench and then held me in place by my shoulders. In my shock, I let her.

"You're stinking up the lunch room with your shitty, old

lady underwear smell," she'd said and shoved me roughly forward. She had been trying to get my face into my tray of food. I had resisted her. Easily. I'd caught a brief flare of surprise on her face and then she tried to shove me one more time.

"Freaks!" she'd said, unable to move me. "Why don't you go somewhere we won't have to smell you?" I had laid my hands on the table and started to stand up, and Evelyn had taken a nervous, compensatory step back.

"Girls!" Mrs. Hamm had said, striding back into the gym. "What's going on here?"

She had hurried across the room, sneakers squeaking, brown sweater wafting her cigarette smell across the tables. Evelyn had put one hand casually on my shoulder in a gesture of friendship. Mimi had come over during the confrontation, drawn by the excitement, and now she used a napkin to help Charity get the globs of food off her clothes. Mrs. Hamm didn't seem to notice that Mimi had also held Charity's arm pinched tightly between two fingers and thumb.

"Somebody threw an apple, and it landed right in Charity's tray!" Evelyn had said, outrage shaking her voice. "Her lunch got all *over* her. Mimi and I came over to help."

Mimi had glanced at Evelyn and from the tucked corners of her mouth; I could see she was barely able to suppress her giggles. I hated them both.

"Okay, who threw the apple?" Mrs. Hamm had asked,

turning to take in the entire room. Even the kids who were not in our class seemed to know better than to speak up. Evelyn had given someone the finger and cursed; that was practically against the law. You could see the astonishment and fear in almost every pair of eyes.

Mrs. Hamm had shaken her head, looking down at Charity. "Well," she'd said, "it was probably an accident." She had looked around, uncertainly. "Okay, no more roughhousing," she'd said, her voice trailing off.

It occurred to me that if it had been another child, she might have been more upset and more eager to find the culprit. But, because it was Charity, her attitude seemed to be that it was better to leave well enough alone.

"Okay, everyone, finish up. It's almost time for you to go back to class," she'd clapped her hands once and started to the kitchen, casting a final glance at Charity as she left.

When Mrs. Hamm had squeaked away, Mimi dropped the napkin full of sticky cheese and macaroni back into Charity's lap and turned from her, giggling in a breathy, strangled way. Evelyn had patted the top of my head and then slapped me on the back, trying to rock me forward.

"Good little Freaky-freak," she'd said. She said it in the crooning, sing-song voice she had used before Mrs. Hamm showed up, but now she was rubbing her hand–it seemed she'd hurt it when she slapped me.

She had sneered at me, a twisted quirk of her thin, pale

lips. "No talking, right, Freakie-freak? You better keep it that way. Or it will get a lot worse for you."

She'd cast a baleful glance at Charity and stalked away, Mimi trotting after like a small, loyal dog, still choking out strangled-sounding giggles.

Charity had still been crying. Big tears had leaked from her eyes, but she'd brushed them away almost as soon as they appeared. She'd begun dabbing at the mess on her shirt and skirt. A swatch of orange had colored her cheekbone. I'd reached across and wiped the dried cheese from her face, my hand shaking. I was trembling from delayed response.

Usually, when I *checked* on Charity, the part of her that exists in my mind, I did it when we were physically apart. I'd never really thought about checking on her when we were together; pure intuition seemed to keep us in tune with what the other was feeling when we were together.

But that day, I remember looking at Charity's wet and teary but mostly calm face. I had realized I didn't have an immediate idea of what she was feeling. I was surprised, actually, that she wasn't crying harder.

I had reached into my mind, and then through it, to Charity.

It was like pushing through heavy curtains, velvet or something even richer than velvet, a fabric impossibly supple but still dense. It felt like the flank of a large, hairless animal, warm and soft, tough but yielding. I could almost feel a heartbeat, a pulse. There was no color, no light, only my hands on ancient softness, my breath easy in this peaceful space.

The small (charity) I found there was calm, not upset at all. I saw her, performing the same tasks as Charity in the world, but the sense I got was one of serenity, and then I understood. Charity thought that would be the end of it. That's why she hadn't been upset. She thought the worst had come and gone and now things would go back to normal.

I had dropped the curtain and retreated back to the real world. Children were taking their trays to the trashcans and filtering out into the hall. I had hoped Charity was right, that the abuse would stop. Maybe Evelyn had had her fill and proved herself enough to the other kids that she'd be content to leave us alone. I hoped so.

I really did.

***

The preceding was the beginning of:
Faith Creation, All Lies Revealed
Book One in the Faith Series
by Christine Dougherty

Available now.
Look for *Faith* on your preferred format or on Amazon for the paperback.

Christine Dougherty

Christine Dougherty is at home in South Jersey
with her husband, dog, and two cats. Visit her at:
www.christinedoughertybooks.com

11227394R00162

Made in the USA
Charleston, SC
08 February 2012